Archibald Campbell

**Lexiphanes**

A Dialogue

Archibald Campbell

**Lexiphanes**
*A Dialogue*

ISBN/EAN: 9783337225780

Printed in Europe, USA, Canada, Australia, Japan

Cover: Foto ©Andreas Hilbeck / pixelio.de

More available books at **www.hansebooks.com**

# LEXIPHANES,

A

# DIALOGUE.

Imitated from Lucian, and fuited to the prefent Times.

### WITH

A Dedication to Lord Lyttleton, a Preface, Notes, and Poftfcript.

### BEING

An attempt to reftore the English Tongue to its ancient Purity,

And to correct, as well as expofe, the affected Style, hard Words, and abfurd Phrafeology of many late Writers, and particularly of

Our English Lexiphanes, the Rambler.

> Whofe ordinary rate of Speech
> In Loftinefs of Sound is rich;
> A *Babylonifh* Dialect,
> Which learned Pedants much affect :
> It is a parti-colour'd Drefs,
> Of patch'd and py-ball'd Languages :
> 'Tis Englifh cut on *Greek* or *Latin*,
> Like Fuftian heretofore on Sattin.
>
> Hudibras.

---

## LONDON:

Printed for, and Sold by J. Knox in the Strand,

MDCCLXVII.

To the RIGHT HONOURABLE

# G E O R G E,
## L O R D  L Y T T L E T O N.

MY LORD,

ON looking round me, throughout the world, for fome diftinguifh-ed character, to whofe protection and foftering care, I might commit the following performance, which ftands fo greatly in need of it, not only as it is the production of a namelefs author, but becaufe it combats many invete-rate prejudices of the age and nation we live in, and likewife attacks fome reputations eftablifhed fo firmly in the opinions of moft men, that they may be thought in no danger from any, I

could

could think of no one to whom I could
addrefs it with fo much propriety as to
your Lordfhip.    And that for feveral
reafons.    In the firft place, your Lordfhip is the beft and happieft imitator of
Lucian our nation has yet produced, and,
you have, with a peculiar felicity, hit off
the natural air and turn of his dialogue.
In the next place, of a learned and a-
nimated writer as your Lordfhip undoubtedly is, you are the pureft and
chafteft of any I know now living, and
the remoteft from that affectation and
*Lexiphanicifm* which are at once the
difgrace and characteriftick of the age.
Therefore it was moft natural for me,
an humble follower of our common and
and great original, and a declared ad-
vocate for the purity and fimplicity of
language, to pitch upon your Lordfhip
for a Patron, who are the beft imitator of the one, or rather a moft beautiful original in a path he has only fhewn
you, and give in your admirable writings, the beft example of the other.

But

' But there was another confideration, which at the time influenced me even more than this, and made me think the prefent addrefs, not only a matter of propriety in regard to myfelf, but alfo a fort of debt or attonement due to your Lordfhip. I beg leave to explain myfelf. I have been all my life-time very little converfant with authors that can ftrictly be called modern; (for even Swift is now to be looked upon as a kind of ancient) and I reckon it my great happinefs to have been fo. I had indeed heard, for who that dabbles in books has not, of the EXCEL-LENT RAMBLER, the *great Mr. S-----l J-----n*; I had likewife feen his volumes on a bookfeller's counter, or a friend's table; and had fometimes taken them up with an intention to perufe a paper or fo, but was never able to go through the tafk, for being prefently difgufted with the pedantry and affectation in every page, I could

not

not help throwing them down with a
contempt and indignation, which, perhaps, the defects of the language ex-
cepted, might be very undeferved.
At laft, during a long voyage at fea,
when I had accefs to no other Englifh
books but what I had been long acquainted and very familiar with, excepting the Ramblers which happened
accidently to be on board, in order to
divert the idle and folitary hours unavoidable in that fort of life, I was, in a
manner obliged to read them, which
accordingly I did with great care and
attention.  I immediately perceived,
and was very forceably ftruck with the
ftrong refemblance there fubfifts between Mr. J----n's character, and that
of the Limoufin fcholar in Rabelais,
and of Lexiphanes in Lucian.  And I
concluded, that an imitation of the latter would be admirably well fuited to
expofe that falfe tafte and ridiculous
manner of writing; and that it might
alfo

alſo be of eminent uſe to letters, by de-
crying that abſurd *Lexiphanick* ſtile,
which from the great and univerſal reputation this Pedant enjoyed, I reaſon-
ably imagined had became faſhionable
among us, and might, in a ſhort time,
bring on an entire decline and corruption, nay, a total alteration of our language, as had been the caſe with the
Roman tongue under the Emperors.

Therefore, as ſoon as I had an opportunity, I ſet about the following work
with all the diligence and application I
was maſter of. In the courſe of it, beſides Mr. J----n's, I carefully peruſed,
it may ſafely be ſaid, for the firſt time,
what other modern writings came in
my way; and I generally found them
more or leſs *Lexiphanick* in proportion
to the ſhare of fame and reputation their
ſeveral authors enjoyed. I now recol-
lected, that your Lordſhip had written
*Dialogues of the Dead*, in imitation of
Lucian, and that I had heard them
b 4                high-

highly applauded. I hope your Lordſhip will forgive me, for I can hardly forgive myſelf, if I concluded, not
having then read them, that thoſe ap-
plauſes might be owing, partly to their
author's quality and exalted ſtation, but
much more to their *Lexiphaniciſm*, or
being written in compliance with the
reigning taſte of the times. I was ambitious, like the yonng Aſcanius, who,
hunting with his father Eneas and Dido.

   --- Dari pecora inter inertia votis
Optat aprum, aut fulvum deſcendere
   monte leonem.

I thought your Lordſhip would be a
much nobler objeƈt of Criticiſm, than
even the *great Mr. S----l J----n*, and
if I ſhould not be able to extraƈt a *Rhapſody* from the *Dialogues*, as eaſily as
from the *Ramblers*, at leaſt I hoped to
have the occaſion of referring to them
frequently in the *notes*, and making
*rhetorical flouriſhes* on their author, who
pro-

profeffing to imitate Lucian, had fo imperfectly ftudied that great original, and fo little profited by his excellent Dialogue of Lexiphanes, and his admirable Effay on the beft manner of writing hiftory.

With fuch views, and with fuch expectations, I immediately had recourfe to your Dialogues. But it was not long before I found myfelf greatly difappointed, and difappointed in a moft agreeable manner. Inftead of being able to fhew them, pardon the freedom of the expreffion, as a fort of fcarecrow or beacon, a warning for others to avoid their faults; I perceived they were a model of imitation, a pattern for all to follow; and was foon made fenfible, I muft content myfelf with becoming a diftant and humble imitator of an author, whom, but a few hours before, I thought to have made the object of my criticifms.

But

But if this was a fmall mortification, it was foon followed by a much
more fenfible pleafure.   If I could not
expofe your Lordfhip's writings as a
warning to others, I found I could do
what was much more for my purpofe,
fupport my own opinion by their great
and unqueftioned authority.   The paffage I have in view, is fo appofite to
the fubject in hand, and coincides fo
entirely with my own fentiments, that
I cannot refift the temptation of quot-
ing it, notwithftanding it may be
thought fomewhat improper in an addrefs to your Lordfhip. It is in the Dialogue  between  Pliny the  Elder,  and
Pliny  the  Younger,  where  the  uncle
fays to the nephew,

---- " Your eloquence had, I think,
" the fame fault as your manners : it
" was generally too *affected*. You pro-
" feffed  to  make  Cicero  your  guide
" and  pattern.   But  when  one  reads
" his Panegyrick  upon  Julius Cæfar,
" and

" and your's upon Trajan, the firſt
" ſeems the genuine language of truth
" and nature, raiſed and dignified with
" all the majeſty of the moſt ſublime
" Oratory : the latter appears the ha-
" rangue of a florid *Rhetorician* ; more
" deſirious to *ſhine*, and to ſet off his
" own wit,. than to extol the great
" man whoſe virtues he was praiſing."

The other makes the following anſwer :

" I will not queſtion your judgment,
" either of my life or my writings.
" They might both have been better,
" if I had not been too ſolicitous to
" render them perfect. It is, per-
" haps, ſome excuſe for the affectation
" of my ſtyle, that it was the faſhion
" of the age in which I wrote. Even
" the eloquence of Tacitus, however
" nervous and ſublime, was not unaf-
" fected. Mine, indeed, was more dif-
" fuſe, and the ornaments of it were
" more tawdry ; but his laboured con-
                                    " ciſeneſs,

" cifenefs, the conftant *glow* of his
" diction, and pointed *brilliancy* of his
" fentences, were no lefs unnatural.
" One principal caufe of this, I fup-
" pofe to have been, that as we de-
" fpaired of excelling the two great
" mafters of Oratory, Cicero and Li-
" vy, in their own manner, we took
" up another, which, to many, ap-
" peared more *fhining*, and gave our
" compofitions a more original air.
" But it is mortifying to me, to fay
" much on this fubject.    Permit me,
" therefore, to refume the contempla-
" tion of that, on which our converfa-
" tion turned before." ----

And here I am forry the nature of
the fubject, which is the famous eruption of Vefuvius, wherein the Elder
Pliny loft his life, prevented your pro-
ceeding any farther.    It might, indeed,
be a mortifying theme to the Panegy-
rift of Trajan, but furely it could not
be fo to the noble author of the Perfian
Let-

Letters, who had in them fhewn fo
fine a tafte, and given fo many illuftrious examples of the natural and fimple
ftyle. I regretted then, and my Lord,
I ftill do regret you had not made it the
fubject of an entire Dialogue. It is well
worthy of your mafterly pen; and befides, you might have rendered it needlefs for an unknown, and what is much
worfe, an inferior hand to undertake
it.

And yet I doubt, whether, upon
fecond thoughts, your Lordfhip's manner be fo well fuited to the adverfaries
you would have to cope withal. For
believe me, as there is not in nature a
vainer, a more felf-fufficient and conceited, fo there cannot be a more unfeeling animal than an old veteran *Lexiphanes*. His fenfations are naturally
fo dull and obtufe, that I queftion much
if he would be in the leaft affected by
the nice touches of your Lordfhip's delicate and refined raillery, fo much like

that

that of Addifon, and of which you have given fo beautiful an illuftration as well as example in the admirable dialogue between Swift and him. Nay, you you have already determined this article againft yourfelf; for in the clofe of that dialogue, where you affign their different provinces to thofe two *rival wits*, you would have " Addifon* employed in comforting thofe whofe delicate minds are dejected with too painful a fenfe of fome infirmities in their nature; and hold up to them his fair and charitable mirrour, which would bring to their fight their hidden excellencies, and put them in a temper fit for Elyfium." And this indeed feems to be the humane and benevolent purpofe of your Lordfhip's work. Whereas to Doctor Swift you " allot the tafk of humbling the arrogant Hero, the vain Philofopher, and the proud Bigot."

But

* Dialogues of the Dead, pag. 32.

But I believe your Lordſhip will agree with me, that the *hard back* of the petulant overbearing Pedant requires as much as any of the other characters, the ſevere laſhes of *that rod, which draws blood at every ſtroke.* It is for this reaſon, ſupported by your great authority, and perhaps from a more cogent one ſtill, it's being better adapted to my own temper and diſpoſition, that I have choſen the rough and coarſer manner of Swift, or rather Lucian.

But to return from this digreſſion, which cannot be altogether impertinent, as moſt of it is taken from your Lordſhip ; I muſt add, that I no ſooner found myſelf deceived, in ſuppoſing you tainted with *Lexiphaniciſm,* which, I need not inform you, literally ſignifies that *ſhining affected diction,* you ſo juſtly condemn, than I determined, ſhould this piece ever be made publick, as a ſmall attonement for the temporary

porary injuſtice I had done you, and
that only in my thoughts, to inſcribe
it to your Lordſhip, and to implore
your protection for it. And as your
high rank and quality would not
have deterred me from criticiſing your
works, had I found occaſion; ſo it is
not that alone, but your great merit
and excellence, your acknowledged
ſuperiority as a writer, that has in a
manner extorted this addreſs from me.
But it has at the ſame time embolden-
ed me, not only to aſk, but even to
expect your patronage and protection.
For after all, my Lord, it is in reality
more your buſineſs than mine. I have
nothing to loſe, I am only a volunteer
in the cauſe, and can hope for nothing,
but a ſmall ſhare of the ſpoil; whereas
you, conſidered as an author, have a
very great eſtate at ſtake; I mean that
honeſt fame, and well deſerved reputation in letters, which I know your

Lord-

Lordſhip muſt have taken ſo much pains to acquire. In ſhort, my Lord, if you at all regard That, you ought not to ſuffer thoſe *Lexiphaneſes,* thoſe *Shiners,* thoſe Dealers in *hard words,* and *abſurd phraſes,* thoſe *Fabricators* of *Triads* and *Quaternions,* and I know not what, to carry all before them in the manner they have lately done, and to perſuade themſelves and the public, that they are the only authors worth regard, and that their uncouth traſh is the ſole ſtandard of perfection in the Engliſh tongue. There is as great an antipathy between a pure and natural writer, ſuch as your Lordſhip, and a Lexiphanes, as there is between an elephant and a rhinoceros. When they meet, they are ſure to fall foul of one another, moſt commonly the Lexiphanes firſt, for the other often holds him too cheap, and the conteſt is never at an end till one is deſtroyed.

c

Be-

Befides, the very circumſtance of your being a man of fortune and quality, will procure you worſe quarter from thoſe Lexiphaneſes, than a meer adventurer would have. The reaſon is this. They are all, excepting the boys juſt raw from the univerſity, authors by profeſſion; and they reckon a gentleman who writes, or in the language of the ſhop, makes a book, an interloper who takes ſo much of their trade out of their hands. They would much rather have his cuſtom than his aſſiſtance in what they all profeſs, the improvement and inſtruction of the reader. They look upon him with no friendlier eyes, than a taylor would on a man of faſhion, who ſhould take a fancy to cut out and make up his own cloaths.

But that they entertain a particular ſpite againſt noble authors, I ſhall give your Lordſhip a very pregnant proof, and ſhew you, from the fate

of

of others, what you have reafon to expect. Highly as I efteem your writings, and though I may think them,
from their moral tendency and the excellent political inftruction contained
in them, of more general benefit than
the productions of either Sheffield, Duke
of Buckingham, or Granville, Lord
Lanfdown; yet, in refpect to elegance
and purity of ftyle, there are few that
can be deemed fuperior. On the contrary, I am affraid, the higheft praife
any modern writer can now reafonably
afpire to, is not to be excelled in thefe
articles by them. And yet that dogmatical Pedant, who is the Hero, or rather
the Butt in the following Dialogue, talking of the fmall damage he imagines
letters have fuftained by the lofs of authors, once famous in their day, com-
forts us, by fuppofing, he does not tell
. us for what reafon, they might be only
the Sheffields and Granvilles of their
times; (I wonder, when his hand was

in, he did not add Clarendon, Temple, Dorfet, in a word, every man of
rank and fortune, who ever put pen to
paper, he might have done it with e-
qual juftice;) and then proceeds very
gravely to inform us, pofterity will
wonder, by what chance or accident,
fuch men ever came to acquire any reputation.

    Thefe Noblemen, my Lord, for the
protection and encouragement they afforded to letters, and for the honour
they did them by their practice and example, were highly and juftly celebrated by all their rival and cotemporary
wits, and by none more than the two
greateft our nation ever produced, Dryden and Pope, one of whom, at leaft,
can never be fufpected of flattery. By
him too your Lordfhip has been greatly
celebrated, for the other was gone long
before you appeared, and yet both have
not faved your predeceffors from the
attacks of this prefumptuous Pedant.

My

My Lord, from the care and polifh-
ing I perceive you have beftowed on
your writings, you muft have been
fomewhat earneft about their fuccefs,
and that reputation you have taken
fuch pains to acquire, you cannot but
wifh to preferve. Nor can you be in-
different about the language of your
native country, that country you love
fo much, of which you are fo bright
an ornament, and whofe excellent conftitution you have illuftrated, explained
and defended, both in your publick and
private capacity with fo great zeal and
fuccefs. But, my Lord, the Ramblers
of Mr. J----n, who has, befides the
advantage of being author of, what is
believed, the only Grammar and Dictionary we yet have, not to mention
many works of others, all in the fame
ftrain, and much applauded and fought
after, are propofed with great confidence to the publick, not only by the
man himfelf, but by his numerous fol-

lowers

lowers and admirers, as the beſt model
ôf writing, and the only ſtandard of
purity and elegance in the Engliſh
tongue ; and what is worſe, are aĉtu-
ally thought to be ſo by nine readers of
ten in the nation.   Hence the queſtion
plainly comes to this reſult.  Whether
we ſhall continue to write and ſpeak
the language tranſmitted down to us
by our anceſtors, who have hardly derived  more  honour  to  their  country,
from their numberleſs viĉtories obtained, and gallant exploits performed
in every quarter of the globe, than
from their inimitable writings in
every branch of ſcience and literature;
or whether we ſhall adopt, I will not
ſay a new language, but a barbarous
jargon, attempted to be impoſed upon
us, by a few School-maſters and Pedants, who owe all their credit to their
petulance and impudence, who are e-
qually ignorant of books and men, and
who think they have done a fine thing
when

when they have tack'd an Englifh termination to a Latin word, and have
huddled together a parcel of quaint unmeaning phrafes, whofe only effect is
to make the ftupid reader ftare, and cry
*'tis mighty fine.*

'Tis true, that in the Dialogue I
have reprefented the overthrow of *Lexiphanicifm* as a very defperate under-
taking indeed. And though this might
be partly done to heighten its humour,
yet I muft confefs, that fuch were in a
great meafure my real fentiments at
the time. But fince, and within thefe
few months, I have feen many late
performances, written in a pure and
manly ftyle, and which I have the
pleafure to fee from the number of
their editions, have met with deferved
fuccefs. From hence, and from fome
other circumftances, I incline, to believe, that *the true tafte* and *Lexiphanicifm*, are at prefent pretty nearly on a
balance, and that an additional weight,

thrown

thrown into the right ſcale, would at once decide the buſineſs. And this weight, none is ſo proper, or has ſo much intereſt to throw in, as your Lordſhip.

Beſides, ſhould the advocates for *plainneſs* and *ſimplicity* be greatly out-numbered by their adverſaries, they are armed with a weapon, which the *Lexi-phaneſes* have not to uſe againſt them, and againſt which, they have at the ſame time no defence. It is not grave, ſolid reaſoning from the genius of our language, the authority of our beſt writers, and ſo forth; for in that caſe, you would ſoon be overpowered by a torrent of hard words and terms of art, which the ignorant multitude would immediately conſtrue into deeper learn-ing. But it is Ridicule. And this powerful engine I have therefore em-ployed againſt them. With what ſuc-ceſs your Lordſhip, and the publick muſt ſoon determine.

But

But should I prove unsuccessful, you, my Lord, whose concern it ought so much to be, can easily recommend the task to another, who may possess happier talents, and perform it in a more satisfactory manner. As for me, I shall account it sufficient honour, to have started the game, tho' I should be thrown out in the chace, and should not even be present at the death.

Having troubled you so long, I must conclude this Address as abruptly as it began, indulging, at the same time, a favourite piece of vanity, by declaring, in this publick manner, that I have the good sense, taste and judgment, to be

Your Lordship's

Sincere Admirer,

And most Obedient

Humble Servant.

P R E-

# PREFACE.

*THE scope and intention of the following performance, is so fully set forth in the Title and Dedication, that little more need be said of it in the preface. But I think it not amiss to inform the Reader, that this Dialogue, together with the* sale of Authors, *and some other imitations of Lucian, was composed about three years ago in one of our American Colonies, as is well known to many in that country. Some friends, and one gentleman in particular, to whom I lay under many other obligations, and perhaps owed both leisure and spirits to resume some long-interrupted and well-nigh forgotten studies, thought so well of the plan, and approved of the intention so much, that they attempted getting it printed at the time and place where it was first written; and with this view, and at their request, I put it in the state it now is. How this attempt came not to succeed, is immaterial, and I only mention it, because some things seem to have*

*been*

*been written for that time, and some authors are taken notice of, who though since dead, were then at the height of their reputation.*

*I had also begun and made some progress in a preface wherein I endeavoured to account for the late manifest decline of taste and good writing among us, and to propose some remedies for the same. But finding I had not lights sufficient to execute such a task as it ought to be, and that were it so done, it would be much too large for the work it was intended to introduce into the world, I left it unfinished; and now find that what I had written is entirely lost, owing to some of those many accidents unavoidable in a wandering unsettled life. I wonder, indeed, the following papers escaped the same fate, having been carelessly tost about, and altogether neglected by me for above two years past. I doubt not but Lexiphanes's janizaries and admirers may very wittily suggest, it would have been no damage if they had; be this however as it may, on revising them now for the press, I chose to let them go as I found them, with the addition of only a few notes. Not that I would hereby insinuate, I think them faultless; on the contrary, I am afraid the Rhapsody is rather too*

*long,*

*long, and even, that it is not so highly finished
as it ought to be, that is to say, it is not sufficiently* Lexiphanick, *if I may use the expression. There are, moreover, a few loose passa-
ges in it, which I am sorry may be thought to
require an apology. But they are wrapt up
in such a mist of* hard words, *that to under-
stand them, requires a closer intimacy with
Lexiphanes, than methinks any fine lady ought
to have. Besides, the original is infinitely
more licentious than the copy. This naturally
led me into them at first, but the true reason
why, on a revisal, I retained them, is what
follows. I really thought the applying those*
cant words *and* affected *phrases, in that
sense, was the best way of ridiculing and expo-
sing them, and should this Dialogue ever become any way popular, it would most effectually
banish them out of good company and polite
writing. I own, likewise, that the references
are neither so numerous, nor perhaps so accu-
rate as they might have been. This is owing
to my having lost some scattered loose papers,
wherein, with a great deal of pains and labour, I had marked down, with their proper
references of pages and numbers, most of the
absurdities I met with on perusing Mr. J----n's
works,*

*works, and some others of the like strain, and from thence had transferred them, as I thought they would come in best into the* Rhapsody, *and those other parts of the Dialogue where* Lexiphanes *is the speaker. There was no other way to remedy this loss, if it really be one, than to go through the same most irksome task over again. But I could not prevail on myself to do it. Truth was, I did not care to be raking any more among their filth and trash, for fear some of it might stick to myself. For in this work, I am no other than a literary scavenger; a sort of gentry very necessary to the cleanliness of others, but by no means the cleanliest folks in the world themselves.*

*As to the rest of the Dialogue, which is, indeed, the principal part, and wherein I have endeavoured to shew, as well as my poor abilities would permit me, both by precept and example, how to write better, I freely own, after a very careful examination, whether respecting its conduct, stile, or sentiments, I do not find any thing I can alter, at least, for the better: and I therefore abandon it as lawful booty to the Criticks to use it as they please.*

*Should it be asked why I have published it, with the imperfections I confess it hath. I*

*an-*

*anſwer, that though this is not deſigned for a
temporary thing, but may laſt and even be uſeful when our Lexiphaneſes are forgotten, yet
it's ſuccefs, and what is pretty odd, it's own
reputation depends, in ſome meaſure, on the
greatneſs of thoſe very reputations it is intended to demoliſh and overturn.    A bad and a corrupt taſte is ever ſickle and changing.    Some
new Lexiphaneſes may ſoon ariſe, who, ſhoot-
ing a bolt beyond Mr. J----n, in his Ramblers,
or Mr. Ak--de, in his Pleaſures of Imagination, may deprive them of that fame they certainly never deſerved to enjoy, and at the ſame
time eſtabliſh their own on the ruins.    They
may likewiſe write in a different manner, in a
manner more difficult to hit, and conſequently
to ridicule and expoſe, in which caſe this performance, about which I confeſs to have taken
a good deal of pains, would be, at the very firſt,
no better than that waſte-paper it may come to
be at laſt.    I am afraid it hath loſt ſome of it's
force and propriety already, and the longer it
is delayed, muſt loſe the more.    Beſides, ex-
pecting, at leaſt hoping ſoon to leave this country, to which I may never return, the preſent
might be the only opportunity I ſhould ever
have of printing it, which I was not willing*

to

*to neglect, for with all its faults, I really do
think it may be eminently useful to the publick,
in correcting and setting right the taste of young
writers, and of young gentlemen at the academy and university, who are so naturally led a-
stray by the false glitter of Mr. J-----n's prose,
and the sublime nonsense of Mr. Ak---de's verse.
For there is good reason to believe, that were
the* Ramblers *and* Pleasures of Imagination
*on the one hand, and the* Spectators *and* Dryden's Fables *on the other, the one the most
faulty and affected, the other the best and pu-
rest of all works of their kind, to be ballotted
for as school-books, in an assembly of all the
masters and school-boys of the nation; there is
good reason to believe, I say, that the former
would carry it against the latter, by a majority
of at least ten to one.*

*There has been much talk about* correcting,
improving *and* ascertaining *a* living tongue,
*as well in our own country, as among the
French and Italians. Many great writers,
and if I mistake not, Doctor Swift among the
rest, have thought a Grammar and Dictionary
necessary for that purpose, and have therefore
lamented the want of them. I have declared
my opinion of these in the Dialogue, but shall*
*here*

*here do it more at large. 'Tis certain that a Grammar or Dictionary, if good for any thing, must be compiled or extracted from* good authors ; *but that these again should become necessary, and even indispensible to form, or rather to create* good authors, *appears to me, I confess, something like a* circle *in* logick, *or the* perpetual motion *in mechanicks ; the one a vicious mode of reasoning, and the other a downright impossibility.* 'Tis true, they may be useful to ladies or country squires, to avoid an error in spelling, and now and then a gross blunder or impropriety in speech. *And farther I conceive their utility, however boasted of, does not extend ; unless, indeed, in a dead language, or to a foreigner who studies a living one, in the same manner we are obliged to study Greek or Latin. But an author or an orator, who takes upon him to write or speak to the people in their own tongue, ought to be above consulting them.*

*Besides, if we have recourse to experience and matter of fact, the surest criterion in all such affairs, we shall perceive, that as the want of them has been no loss, so when procured, they have done as little service. Homer and Virgil, Demosthenes and Cicero,*

d         *Thucidides*

*Thucidides and Livy, all wrote without Grammar or Dictionary, and most of them without so much as knowing what they were. So have all the best writers of Italy, France and England. Nor do I hear that the Dictionaries of the two former, though compiled by bodies of men, the most illustrious for their learning, have done any mighty feats since their appearance; that they have fixed or established their respective languages, or made the writers in either, a whit more elegant and correct than they would have been without them. We too, in imitation of them, must also have our Dictionary. But by whom is it compiled? By Lexiphanes himself, the great corrupter of our taste and language. I own I have never had opportunity to consult either the French or Italian Dictionaries; but Mr. J-----n's, I am certain, falls infinitely short of what I conceive it ought to be, to answer any purpose it is pretended to serve. It ought to contain, in a manner, a distinct treatise on every word that is, or ever has been in use, branched out into a thousand particulars very difficult to enumerate, but almost impossible to execute. And what man or body of men are equal to such a task? Besides, were it execu-*

*ted,*

*ted; who could use it, or reap any benefit from it? It would be in itself a library, infinitely more voluminous than the* abridgment *of our* laws *in* twenty Volumes Folio, *or even than our laws themselves at large. In short, we may pronounce a perfect Dictionary to be like the Philosopher's Stone, once a great* Desideratum *among some people, impossible to obtain, and which, perhaps, we are better without.*

*The celebrated Doctor Swift, in his* proposal for correcting, improving, and ascertaining the English Tongue, *strenuously recommends the institution of a society composed* of such persons, as are generally allowed to be best qualified for such a work, *namely, the fixing, correcting, and enlarging our language,* without any regard to quality, party, or profession: and who, to a certain number, at least, should assemble at some appointed time and place, and fix on rules by which they designed to proceed. *That such a society instituted at that time, and composed of persons, appointed by Swift himself, or by the great man to whom the* proposal *is addressed; might have been eminently useful for the purposes* there mentioned, *I shall not, by any means, bring into question. But then, who*

*would*

*would warrant the immortality of thofe perfons;
or that their fucceffors fhould be poffeffed of the
fame abilities, and animated with the fame
fpirit? In that fuppofition, indeed, it is poffible fuch Lexiphanick fuftian, as we have
lately been peftered with, might never have
had exiftence, at leaft, never been heard of.
But in the fituation things now are, I think I
may venture to affert, without any danger of
rafhnefs, that if fuch a fociety had been infti-
tuted a few years ago, and I know not but it
would be the fame at prefent, our great Lexicographer, the excellent Rambler, would have
been elected Secretary, and, perhaps, the Britifh Lucretius, of whom more hereafter, appointed Regifter of it. Then, indeed, matters
would have been much worfe, and really paft
redemption. For who would have been fo
hardy as to attack, and on the fcore of their
language too, the Secretary and Regifter of an
Academy erected for correcting, improving, and
afcertaining that very language; and at the
head of which, moft certainly would have been
every the moft illuftrious name and character
in the nation. Even as the cafe now ftands,
this attempt is, by fome, I know, thought too
daring for a private perfon. Perhaps it may
be*

*be true, that nothing can entirely justify him in it but success ; though, indeed, my perfect indifference, at least, with respect to private concerns, whether it succeed or no, may plead my excuse.*

*Having thus, and I think on very sufficient grounds, rejected as improper aud inadequate every method hitherto proposed, though by some of our greatest men, for the laudable purposes of fixing and ascertaining our Mother Tongue, it may be thought incumbent on me, to propose another which may supply the deficiencies of others. I have already done it in the Dedication. The corrupters of our tongue, in the days of Swift and Steele, were pert lively fops ; they were great curtailers of words, and took a pleasure in lopping off their first and last syllables, as owls bite off the feet of mice, in order to confine and fatten them. But our modern gentry are quite the reverse of the others ; they are grave, solemn, formal coxcombs, and have much more of the ass than the ape in their composition ; they cannot endure an elision, are mighty fond of long-tailed worm-like words, and as they think cur own language does not afford a sufficient stock of them, they import them in great quantities from the Greek and Latin. There-*

*Therefore they are the properest objects of ridi-cule in the world, and though from their stupi-dity, pride, or conceit, they may not smart so severely at first, under the lash, as a livelier dunce; yet it must have a greater and more du-rable effect upon them at last; and whatever fondness they may express in imitation of their Principal for* jocularity and burlesque, harm-lefs merriment, eafy facetiousnefs, and flow-ing hilarity; *yet as they are altogether inca-pable of making a retort, and quite unprovided with any means of defence, they must soon be laught out of all their followers and admirers, and left single and destitute by themselves.*

*There are now, and I trust always will be, many persons of real taste and wit in the nation, and were they to join, in a scheme of this sort, and mutually encourage and sup-port one another in the prosecution of it, they would find it a much more effectual means than all the Dictionaries and Academies in the world, for preventing our language being infected by any species of corruption, particularly that which seems to threaten it most at present.    In a word, whenever a Lexiphanes makes his es-cape from his usual nest or den, a school or a college, and begins to acquire a reputation, to*

*make*

*make a noife in the world, to take upon him, and to treat the reft of mankind as if they were fo many boys, or his pupils ftill trembling under his Ferula, let them inftantly fall upon him as the birds do upon an owl which appears by day-light, and drive him back to his original obfcurity and lurking places; in a word, hunt him down without mercy, as I have endeavoured to do by this* great unlick'd Cub, *who came firft in my way, and is indeed the moft confpicuous of them all.*

# ARGUMENT.

MR. J-----n or the Englifh Lexiphanes and the Critick meet. After fome compliments paft between them, Lexiphanes rehearfcs his Rhapfody. It contains a rant about Hilarity and a Garret; Oroonoko's adventure with a Soldier; his own journey to Highgate, and adventures there and on the road; his return to London, and lawfuit about his horfe; his walk to Chelfea, where he plays at fkittles; his being frightened by a calf on his return, which he miftakes for the Cock-lane Ghoft; his amours and difappointments at a Bagnio. He is now interrupted by the Critick, who takes him to tafk for his hard words and affected ftyle, and thinking him mad, applies to a Phyfician paffing by, who proves to be the Britifh Lucretius. He repeats a great many verfes, and the Critick gets rid of him with fome difficulty. Another Doctor comes up, who is the Critick's friend. They talk together upon Lexiphanes's cafe, and other matters concerning tafte and writing. They force him to fwallow a potion which makes him throw up many of his hard words. The Doctor goes to a confultation, and the Critick inftructs Lexiphanes how to avoid his former faults, and write better for the future.

L E X I-

# LEXIPHANES.

## A

# DIALOGUE.

CRITICK. J - - - - - N. FIRST PHYSICIAN. SECOND PHYSICIAN.

### CRITICK.

SEE J-----N yonder, our Englifh Lexi-phanes, marching along with a huge folio under his arm. Some new piece I'll warrant, in the ftile of his Ramblers. I fhall be well entertained, if he is in a reading humour; a thing he is often fonder of than many of his hearers.

### J - - - - - N.

Moft happily occurred, my very benevo-lent convivial affociate. Behold. A novel exhibition which is purely virginal, and which has never been critically * furveyed by any annual or diurnal retailer of litera-ture, in this fo fignal † a metropolis.

---

* Rambler No. 10. *critically condemned.*

† I beg leave to obferve here once for all, that I do not intend to confine myfelf to a clofe imitation

of

What! a new romance, or a second Raffelas of Abyffinia?

J - - - - ↲ N.

Without dubiety you mifapprehend this dazzling fcintillation of conceit in totality*, and had you had that conftant recurrence to my oraculous dictionary, which was incumbent upon you from the † vehemence of my monitory injunctions, it could not have efcaped you that the word novel exhibits to all men dignified by literary honours and fcientifical accomplifhments, two difcrepant fignifications. The one imports that which

you

of Lexiphanes's manner of writing only, but propofe to fhew by example the abfurdity of hard words, and affectation in general. For inftance, the words *novel* and *fignal* are not much ufed by Lexiphanes, that I remember, but Gordon, in his Tacitus, is mighty fond of them. They are here affected, as they generally are in Gordon, yet have been ufed by fome of our beft writers, though very fparingly. But bad authors have the fame influence on words, that the dregs of the people have upon drefs.

* Rambler, No. 141.

† Raffelas, *vehement injunctions of hafte.* Rambler, No. 26. *monitory letters.*

you have affixed to it, a romance or fiction,
such as the tale of Ajut and Anningait, or
the Prince of Abyssinia ‖, but that in
which I have at present used it, signifies
new, recent, hodiernal. And indeed the
eye of critical discernment will perceive,
that there is a most exquisite elegancy in
conferring that appellation upon a recent
and hodiernal production. But I am afraid
that your intellects are exhausted, * or dis-
torted, † that their fortresses are betray'd to
rebels, and their children excited to sedition,
‡ and that you are now labouring under an
intellectual famine, and want the banquet of
the lady Pekuah's conversation §.

### CRITICK.

Excuse, dear sir, the dullness of my ap-
prehension. But pray what is the subject of
this new piece?

### J ----- N.

It is a rhapsody or a characteristical ef-
say, an assemblage calculated to enhance
and

---

‖ Tales and romances of our author well known.
\* Raff. V. 1. p. 16.    † Ram. No. 95.
‡ Raff. V. 1. p. 120.    § Raff. V. 2. p. 94.

and diverfify convivial feftivity. But you
muft underftand, that I totally anti-rhapfo-
dize Afhley.

CRITICK.

What then! you don't retail your characters in fmall quantities, as Afhley his punch,
*pro bono publico ?* We have them wholefale.
But there are many of that name, and I fhould
rather imagine, as it's a rhapfody, you mean
my Lord Shaftfbury.

J - - - - - N.

You arread me aright. And, indeed,
this * luxuriant efflorefcence of my wit would
have been utterly inexplicable to any but
one of your fagacity of conjecture, acutenefs of comprehenfion, and facility of penetration †. You are one of thofe gigan-

---

* Ram. No. 141.

† This is quite in Lexiphanes's ftyle. He is
mighty fond of ending a fentence with three phrafes
of this fort, for the moft part equally fuperfluous
and igfignificant. When he hath done this, no
doubt he thinks he hath rounded off the period well,
and hath added fomething to the harmony to its cadence. Ram. No. 208. Innumerable examples of
this kind are to be met with in his writings. One I
found in the very paragraph whence I took the laft
quotation

tick and ſtupenduous intelligences who graſp a ſyſtem by intuition *.

### CRITICK.

Well then, give us a ſample of your work, that I may not be altogether deprived of ſo great a feaſt, for I promiſe myſelf it will be as good as a cup of Nectar† .

B 3        J - - - - - N.

quotation. *Colloquial barbariſms, licentious idioms, and irregular combinations.* Ram. 208. Another I met with, as I juſt now caſt my eye on the firſt number of his third volume. *The prejudice of faction, the ſtratagem of intrigue, and the ſervility of adulation.* Ram. No. 106. Theſe may very properly be called *Triads.* But ſometimes, and when he is diſpoſed to be more eloquent than common, he mounts it up to a *quaternion*, of which there are likewiſe many examples in his Ramblers.

* Ram. No. 108. If one could ſuſpect ſuch an original genius as Lexiphanes of being a plagiary, he hath borrowed *graſp a ſyſtem by intuition*, from king Phys, in the Rehearſal, who *graſps a ſtorm with the eye of reaſon.* Akinſide, our poetical, or rather blank-verſe Lexiphanes, has an expreſſion of much the ſame nature,

> When deſpair ſhall graſp
> His agonizing boſom.

Pleaſ. of Imag. b. ii, v. 491.

* Almoſt literal from Lucian.

### J - - - - - N.

Deject then † exaggeratory obloquy below the horizon of your profpects, ‡ without the fervility of adulation afford open-
nefs of ears, fedulity of thought, and ftabi-
lity of attention §.   But above all ‖ expulfe
hereditary aggregates  and  agglomerated
afperities which may obumbrate  your intellectual luminaries with the clouds of obfcurity, or obthurate the porches of your intelligence with  the  adfcititious  excrement of
critical malevolence.

### C R I T I C K.

Begin boldly,  my good friend,  there are
neither agglomerated afperities nor hereditary aggregates about me*.

### J - - - - - N.

Confider well how  I  have conglomerated
this atchievement of erudition, the infinua-
tion

---

† Raffelas.          ‡ Ram. No. 2.
§ Here's another Triad *more Lexiphanice.*
‖ Gordon's Tacitus.

* In the place anfwering this, in the original,
Lucian tells Lexiphanes, that he has no vermin a-
bout him, neither lice nor fleas ; a play upon words
which it was impoffible to preferve in the copy.

tion of its exordial fentences, the felection of its diction, and refplendency of its fentiment.

### CRITICK.

It muſt be all that, if yours. But I pray you begin *.

B 4                    J - - - - - N.

* What goes before is a pretty cloſe copy of Lucian, the ſame conceits and playing upon words as near as the different turn of the two languages would allow. For inſtance, Lexiphanes tells Lucian, that he antiſympoſiaẓes Ariſto, which was Plato's original name, but by which he was little known. In the ſame manner J————n tells the Critick, who, in this dialogue, acts the part of Lucian, that he anti-rhapſodizes Aſhley, a name, at leaſt, never uſed when one ſpeaks of my Lord Shaftſbury. Lucian's Lexiphanes is a pert conceited fop, whereas mine, like his living original, is a grave ſolemn affected pedant and coxcomb. Lucian's Sympoſium, as far as we can now know of the matter, is an original. But my Rhapſody is moſtly taken from the Ramblers with ſome few quotations and parodies from the Elements of Criticiſm, Night-Thoughts, Pleaſures of Imagination, Centaur not Fabulous, and Warton's Eſſay on Pope. Lucian has jumbled together a parcel of the ſtrangeſt incoherent ſtuff and nonſenſe that can well be imagined. I hope I have equall'd him in this point, however ſhort I may have fallen in other articles.

J - - - - - N.

I fhall inchoate with one of it's moft delicious morfels of eloquence, and fhall at the
fame time be curt*.    Perpend†, and receive
my fayings with a ftedfaft ear‡.    But I obfecrate that in the interim you would, by a
proper feceffion, facilitate my enjoyment of
the light, whilft I, by the fortuitous lique-
faction of fpectacular lenfes, and their con-
cordant adaptation to my temporal regions,
meliorate and prolong its fruition §.

" After

* Elements of Criticifm.
† Piftol in Shakefpear.
‡ Pleaf. of Imag.   B. 2. L. 306.
§ 'Tis fuppofed that in this fentence Lexiphanes
means no more than that the critic fhould ftep afide
while he puts on his fpectacles.   For fome of the hard
words, and quaint phrafes, confult Rambler, No. 9.
And now Lexiphanes begins to read his Rhapfody,
conceived in the following words : *After our poft-
meridional refection, rejoined Hypertatus, &c.* and continues reading till interrupted by the critic   The
fragment here given, without either beginning or
ending, is fuppofed to be only a fmall  part of a
larger work; for Mr. J-----n tells us, he *inchoates
with one of its moft delicious morfels of criticifm.*  Lucian begins and ends his Sympofium in the fame
abrupt manner, and though it be in itfelf a matter
of perfect indifference, I thought it better to follow
the example of fo great an original.

" After our poft-meridional refection, rejoined Hypertatus, we will regale with a
fupernumerary compotation of convivial ale,
fo adapted to exhilarate the young, and animate the torpor of hoary wifdom with fallies
of wit, burfts of merriment, and an unintermitted ftream of jocularity. From this
affemblage of feftivity we will unanimoufly
extrude thofe fcreech-owls whofe only care
is to crufh the rifing hope, to damp the kind-
ling tranfport, and allay the golden hours
of gaiety with the hateful drofs of grief and
fufpicion. Such is Sufpirius, whom I have
now known fifty-eight years and four
months, who has intercepted the connubial
conjunction of two hundred and twenty fix
reciprocal hymeneal folicitors by prognof-
tications of infelicity, and has never yet
paffed an hour with me in which he has not
made fome attack upon my tranquillity, by
reprefenting to me, that the imbecillities of
age, and infirmities of decrepitude are coming faft upon me. Indeed to thofe whofe
timidity of temper fubjects them to extemporaneous impreffions, who fuffer by fafcination, and catch the contagion of mifery,
it is extreme infelicity to live within the
compafs

compass of a screech-owl's voice. Therefore let us avoid Suspirius with a studied sedulity, and should we fortuitously meet him
in the multifarious confluxes of men, let us
repress the solicitude of his advances with a
frigid gracioufness*.

" We shall likewise emancipate our convivial affociation from Mr. Frolick, that dif-
feminator of the knowledge of what is echo-
ed in the streets of London, who takes advantage of reverential modesty with despo-
tick and dictatorial powers of prescribing,
and impofes upon rustick underftandings
with a falfe exhibition of univerfal intelligence, catches of interruption, brifknefs of
interrogation, and pertnefs of contempt †.
He thinks us unworthy of the exertion of
his powers, or his faculties are benumb'd
by rural ftupidity, as the magnetick needle
lofes its animation by approximating the po-
lar

---

* For moft of the hard words, quaintneffes, and
abfurdities of ftyle in this paragraph, confult the
character of Sufpirius the fcreech-owl, in the Rambler, No 59.

† For the *delicious morfels of eloquence*, and choice
flowers of fpeech in this and the next paragraph, fee the characters of Meff. Frolick and Philomides, Rambler, No. 61, 72.

lar climes. Therefore we shall treat him with rustick sincerity, and drive him as an impostor to regions of more credulity.

" But Philomides shall be welcome to us, who possesses good humour, that subaltern endowment, which is the balm of being, a perennial mollitude of manners, facility of approach, and suavity of disposition.

" We shall also have the company of Hilarius who enjoys a flattering and alluring superiority conferred by the powers of conversation, an extemporaneous sprightliness of fancy, and fertility of sentiment. He has applied his faculties to jocularity and burlesque, and his imagination is heated to such a state of activity and ebullition, that on every occasion it fumes away in evaporations of gaiety, and never fails to kindle up a blaze of merriment. Nor shall we even refuse the association of * Gelasimus, who, though his priority is not acknowledged, was the first who gave a full explication of all the properties of the Catenarian curve. His merit introduced him to splendid tables, where he was entangled in many ceremonial perplexities from which all his dia-

grams

* Ram. No. 179.

grams could not extricate him, and was
fometimes engaged with female difputants
with whom his algebraick axioms had
no great weight, and to whom he was very
little recommended by his theory of the
tides, and approximations to the quadrature
of the circle. Nor wanted Gelafimus penetration to difcover that no charm was more
generally irrefiftible than that of eafy facetioufnefs and flowing hilarity. He therefore
came to a fudden refolution of throwing off
the cumbrous ornaments of learning, and
commencing a man of wit and jocularity.
Though utterly unacquainted with every
topick of merriment, yet he never fails to
laugh whenever he ftirs the fire, fills a glafs,
removes a chair, or fnuffs a candle, as laughter he knows is a token of alacrity. Thus
his rifibility will be kept in inceffant exercitation by Hilarius's powers of delighting.
He will even afford a topick of merriment
himfelf, for thofe who defire to partake of
the pleafure of wit, muft contribute to its
production, fince the mind ftagnates without external ventilation, and that efflorefcence of the fancy, which flafhes into
　　　　　　　　　　　transport,

tranfport, can be raifed only by the infufion of diffimilar ideas *.

"Then, when we fhall have received a fufficient ftream of pofterior invigoration, and elevated our powers to a due animation, by the quaffing of our convivial ale, we will refrigerate with an ambulatory circumrotation in the Park, and return homewards with the corufcations of declining day. For the feafon of the year is now come in which the regions of luxury are for a while unpeopled, and pleafure leads forth her votaries to groves and gardens, to ftill fcenes, and erratick gratifications. For I cannot but fufpect, that this month, bright with funfhine and fragrant with perfumes; this month which covers the meadow with verdure, and decks the gardens with all the mixtures of colorifick radiance; this month from which the man of fancy expects new infufions of imagery, and the naturalift new exhibitions of obfervation; this month will congeal multitudes into a ftate of hopelefs wifhes and pining recollection, where the

eye

---

* For the hard words and affected phrafes in this paragraph, confult the characters of Gelafimus and Hilarius in the Rambler.

eye of vanity will, in vain, look round for
admiration, and the hand of avarice ſhuffle-
cards, in a bower, with inefficacious dex-
terity *.

"In relation to myſelf, I will recede to
my garret. For the gaiety and ſprightlineſs
of dwellers, in elevated regions, is probably
owing to the encreaſe of that vertiginous
motion with which we are carried round by
the diurnal revolution of the earth. The
powers of agitation upon the ſpirits are well
known, and nothing is plainer, than that he
who towers to the fifth ſtory, is whirled
through more ſpace by every circumrotation,
than another that grovels upon the ground
floor. Indeed, I think a frequent removal
to various diſtances from the center ſo neceſſary to a juſt eſtimate of intellectual abilities, that I would propoſe that there ſhould
be a cavern dug, and a tower erected like
thoſe which Bacon deſcribes in Solomon's
houſe, for the expanſion and concentration
of underſtanding, according to the exigence

of

* The above rant is, I believe, taken almoſt
word for word from the Rambler, though, for
want of a good Index, I cannot at preſent point out
the number.

of different employments or conftitutions. Perhaps, fome that fume away in meditations on time and fpace in the tower, might compofe tables of intereft at a certain depth, and he, that upon level ground, ftagnates in filence, or creeps in narrative, might, at the height of half a mile, ferment into merriment, fparkle with repartee, and froth with declamation. I have difcovered, by a long feries of obfervations, that invention and elocution fuffer great impediments from denfe and impure vapours, and that the tenuity of a defecated air, at a proper diftance from the furface of the earth, accelerates the fancy, and fets at liberty thofe intellectual powers which were before fhackled by too ftrong attraction, and unable to expand themfelves under the preffure of a grofs atmofphere. I have found dullnefs to quicken into fentiment in a thin ether, as water not over-hot boils in a receiver partly exhaufted, and heads to appearance empty, have teemed with notions on rifing ground, as the flaccid fides of a football would have fwelled out into ftiffnefs and erection. All which perhaps, I may reveal to mankind

kind in a treatife on barometrical pneu-
matology§."

" Thus concluded Hypertatus his elaborate diſſertation on convivial Ale, Hilarity,
Merriment, and a Garret. He then ſhewed
me a moſt encomiaſtick veneration, overwhelmed me with a luſcioufneſs of eulogy,
and beſtowed on me magnificent remuneratory honours *, for the prime radical excel-
encies, perſpicacity of remarks, and verſatile
plaſtick imagination † diſplayed in my Ramblers, which, on that account, he imagined, when I compoſed them, I had quitted

my

§ In order to underſtand the beauties of this paragraph, conſult Hypertatus's letter to the Rambler,
upon the conveniencies and advantages of a Garret.
This is one of Mr. J-----n's *chef d'œuvres,* both for
ſtile and matter. Befides, which is not very frequent
with him, he makes an attempt in this place at wit
and humour, but with his uſual ſucceſs. Of this
however more hereafter.

Hitherto Hypertatus, Mr. J-----n's friend and
correſpondent, is ſuppoſed to be the ſpeaker in the
Rhapfody; and the praiſes of *convivial* ale, *hilarity,*
*merriment,* and a *garret* are all put in his mouth.
Lexiphanes himſelf relates from henceforth what
follows in his own perſon.

* Rambler, No. 104.
† Warton's Eſſay on Pope.

my garret, and afcended into the cock-
loft. He called me EXCELLENT
RAMBLER∥!

" Afterwards he requefted me to accom-
pany him in his ambulatory projects, but I
tranfmitted him a declinature ‡ on account
of the pain which I fuffered from fome artificial excoriations which I had contracted
on a very refpectable part of my body, by
the fevere fuccuffations of a conductitious
fteed when I was taking a tollutation to Highgate.

" I had laid the stricteft monitory injunctions on Oroonoko, my fwarthy boy of
Ethiopian race, to hie before as my precur-
for *, and befpeak a vefpertine collation at
a Caravanferay, whofe mafter was moft renown'd for culinary fcience and economical
accomplifhments. But the Renegado dif-
obeyed my moft abfolute commands, and as
he was paffing through Field-Lane, his olfactory powers being affected by odoriferous
fteams, lured him to linger in the fhops of

C                   culinary

∥ Warton's Effay on Pope.
‡ Robertfon's Hiftory of Scotland, Vol. 2d. See
the ftory of *Mas David Black.*
* Warton, ut fupra.

culinary retailers, and banquet upon favory fheep's heads, prime pigs pettytoes, and plump plumb-pudding. His powers of manducation and digeftion being now fatiated; and being fatisfied of my firm adherence to a rational and equitable adaptation of penalties to offences, and under no terror of death, the ftrongeft and moft operative of prohibitory fanctions †, the thirfty fever that raged in his throat, hurried him, with all the ardor of precipitation, to the fign of the man arrayed in vernal livery. Replete with pecuniary impudence, from having withheld the change of a quarter image of our moft amiable fovereign, which I had yefterday given him in order to acquire a faufageary refection with an intention of refufcitating and invigorating my powers which were languid and debilitated with fedulity of application in abftracting an octavo from my folio dictionary, he fat down on a bench fuccumbing under laffitude and indigeftion, called for beer with all the vociferation of impatience, and thus began :

> T' inebriate at brifk porter's fountain head,
> And reeling thro' the wildernefs of joy ;
>
> Where

† Ram. No. 114.

Where senfe runs favage, broke from rea-
    fon's chain,
And fang falfe peace.

Night Thoughts.

" For, behold, on a vicinary bench, fate a
plunder-fed * foldier, between whom and
Oroonoko, in the courfe of the vivacious loquacity of their evening compotations † a-
rofe an unextinguifhable feud, a mutual vi-
gilance to entrap, and eagernefs to deftroy,
a continual exacerbation of hatred, and inceffant reciprocation of mifchief ‡. This
Thrafo affuming a faftidious tumour of dignity, with negative rudenefs and obliquities
of infult, effufed his invidious farcafms, and
defcants on the negro darknefs of Oroonoko, who now verging towards a ftate of in-
ebriation, his intellects became diftorted
with argumental delirium, the controverfy
was foon inflamed to the higheft pinnacle of
exacerbation, and then he beftowed reiterated percuffions on the intellectual regions of
this plunder-fed foldier. Thus commenced

C 2　　　　　　a cir-

---

* Blackwell, court of Auguftus.
† Ram. No. 133, 141.
‡ Ram. No. 185.

a circulatory war *. The foldier effayed to refift, but in vain, for he was foon neceffitated to fuccumb, if not under the mental, at leaft under the manual fuperiority of Oroonoko. The breaft of this difcomfited militant was now corroded with envy, for which, when it has attained its height, perhaps, no remedy will be found in the gardens of philofophy: however, fhe may boaft her phyfick of mind, her catharticks of vice, or lenitives of paffion †. He willingly fuffered the corrofions of inveterate hatred, and gave up his thoughts to the gloom of malice, and the perturbations of ftratagem. In curt, he applied to a prefs-gang then in the vicinity, and got Oronooko conveyed into a tender, from which I relieved him not, till after frequent folicitations and many fruftraneous applications of intereft.

" Thus was I conftrained to take a folitary excurfion. Moreover my palfrey was fpavinated, fo that being compelled to flog and calcitrate with all the ardour of impatience, he agitated me with fuch fevere and defultory commotions, that I fuffered a total perineal

---

* Gordon's Tacitus.    † Ram. No. 2.

rineal excoriation, which not emollients could medicate, the powers of medicine alleviate, nor the skill of physicians elude.     But this, my sole misfortune, at that time was not *. The spavination of my steed being now meliorated by the warmth † of exercitation; and by the due alternate application of the curbing, flogging and spurring powers, having reduced him to an equable and moderate equitation, I continued tollutating along with the most placid tranquillity, meditating the subject of a vernal speculation. But all of a sudden, my powers of attention were arrouzed, my meditations suspended, and my concatenation of seminal ideas totally dissipated by a violent conquassation of the umbrageous foliage above, and a manifest concussion of the earth below.     'Tis, indeed, wonderful, as with all the powers of descriptive poetry, the British Lucretius ‡ expresses it,

* *War at that time there was none.* Thus Gordon, the first affected author, who seems to have met with encouragement from our great men, chuses to translate the following very simple passage in Tacitus. *Nullum ea tempestate bellum.*

† Vid. Lucian.

‡ Some of Mr. J——'s friends may here object,

With what accumulated force,
Th' impetuous nerve of paffion urges on
The native weight and energy of THINGS.
Pleaf. of Imagination.

" The caufe of this convulfive motion in
nature, was a congrefs between a bard of fignal celebrity, and one of thofe nymphs who
enjoy a perpetual fufceptibility of occafional
de-

jeft, that his fentiments, with refpeft to this poet,
are mifreprefented, and that no where in his writings hath he either commended him or called him
the Britifh Lucretius. But I anfwer, that I am as
far from imputing to him any of the opinions ad-
vanced in this Rhapfody, as I am from fathering
upon him any of the adventures contained in it.
'Tis a fufficient warrant for me, if fome authors of
note in the world have praifed Ak——e, and ftiled
him our Lucretius. Befides, I have not thar defpi-
cable notion of Mr. J ———'s tafte, efpecially in
poetry, fome people affeft to have. If we may
judge of it, from what he hath himfelf done in that
way, he muft defpife the other as heartily as I do.
His imitations of Juvenal are truely excellent, and
as much fuperior to the pleafures of imagination, as
the Ramblers are inferior to the Tatlers and Spefta-
tors. The truth is, Mr. J ——— n has too much
good fenfe to admire, and too great fkill in the *politicks of literature* to applaud any body's nonfenfe
but his own,

delight. They were in the height of the complicated joy, eagerly co-operating and mutually accelerating the intended event *, juſt as I happened to be ambling along. My ſteed alarmed and terrified at theſe tumultuary phenomena, alternately plunged down his head, reared up on his poſteriors, and at laſt dejeĉted me with a headlong precipitation into a muddy ditch, and then, with an incredible acceleration of velocity, vertiginated along the arable, impregnated with a grain, which in England feeds the horſes, but in Scotland ſupports the people †. Annihilation and exiſtence were now

* Eſſay on Pope. Elem. of Criticiſm.

† The above is the definition given of oats by Lexiphanes in his very facetious diĉtionary, and is, no doubt, intended by him for a farcaſm againſt the Scotch; a people he is ſaid to hold in high contempt, and, in my opinion, very juſtly too, for moſt of them, I have been told, are his great admirers, and ſo much his very humble ſervants, that they think it even an honour to be abuſed by him. For my own part, the more I ſtudy this exalted genius, the more I am forced to admire him. For inſtance, one ſhould naturally expeĉt wit and humour in periodical Eſſays, Novels, and Romances; but read his Ramblers and Raſſelas, you meet with nothing like it, nothing but what he calleth, *ſtern philoſophy,*

*dolour*

fo nearly equiponderant, that they lay in the trepidations of the balance. I rifqued a fubaqueous voyage *, a total interruption of reciprocal refpiration, a † comminution of life, in curt, a forisfamiliation out of the univerfe. But our poet's powers of commiferation being arrouzed at fuch a compaffionable objeƈt as I then exhibited, fuffered not his ardour for a reciprocation of pleafures and multiplying ftipulations to preponderate over his feelings of humanity. He hied with all the ardour of folicitude to deliver me from thofe ftagnated waters of collefted impurity, where a frigorifick torpor had already begun to encroach on my veins.

dolourous declamation, and dictatorial inftruction: whereas confult his dictionary, and there you have it with a vengeance. In fhort, he is author of the firft witty dictionary that ever was heard of. This, however, is not all. Befides, being witty and facetious, 'tis alfo national, perfonal, political, and patriotical; in a word, every thing but what it ought to be. For proof of which, befide the aforefaid article of oats, confult his definitions of Excife, Favourite, Gazetteer, Penfion, Penfioner, Revolution, &c.

* Ram. No. 109.
† Ram. No. 108. Elem. of Criticifm.

veins*. He ftoop'd fublime †, and at laft re-
inftated me, and when my powers of obfervation were refufcitated, exhibited an unu-
fual appearance to my view. A ruddy plenilunar refplendant countenance, a vigorous
athletick herculean form, arrayed in a rufty
black coat, and dirty buck-fkin breeches.
Senfible of the univerfality of the caufe of
my prefent infelicities, I rouzed up all my
particular powers of dolorous declamation,
and warbled my groans with uncommon
elegance and energy ‡. I effufed the following ejaculation againft the whole fpecies of
nymphs who enjoy a perpetual fufceptibility
of occafional delight §.

"May Lais, Thais, Limax, Lupa, Succu-
ba, Quadrantaria, Obolaria, Euriole, Sthe-
nio, Medufa, Erinnys, Megæra and Tyfi-
phone. --- May all thefe, and all fuch ladies,
whether fick or found, high or low, of blood
and title, or ditch and dunghill, natives foreign or infernal. --- May this glorious group
of

* See Nouradin, the merchant's dying addrefs to
his fon Almamoulin.  Ramb. Vol. 3. p. 80.
† Pleaf. Imag. B. 2. L. 268.
‡ Ramb. No. 109.
§ Ramb. No. 111.

of Torrifmond's angels, thefe Gorgons furies, harpies, leaches, Syrens, centaur making
ing Syrens! paid or unpaid, keeping or
kept, on fire or quenched, genevaed or ci-
troned, in clofet or cellar, in tavern, bagnio, brothel, roundhoufe, bridewell, or new-
gate. --- Oh may they ceafe, from this hour,
to fing or dance, fmile or frown, pleafe or
plague, pray or fwear, our Britifl, unbri-
tifh youth, manhood or age, out of their
fenfes, health, eftates, reputation, human
nature, and hopes of heaven!

" And thefe enchantreffes laying afide their
fpells, may the bewitched of Great-Britain
recover their priftine form, as Circe's herd,
at the prayer of Ulyffes. At the touch of
my difenchanting pen, may they leap out of
their hides for joy; and laying hold on
their long deferted definition of man, reafon and two legs, walk uprightly for the
future.

" Rejoice with me, my friend! for do I
dream, or didft thou not obferve? Didft
thou not hear? Intonuit lævum. As the
dark cloud which caufed it is vanifhed, and
a flood of light rufhes in; fo fhall it fare
with thee; I fee thy dawning reafon; I fee
                                          the

the break of thy moral day. And what I fee, I fhall relate; and what I relate, tho' ftrange, let no man difbelieve *.

" Concluding thus my ejaculation, the bard rejoined.

Ah! what, my friend, has private life to do
With things of public nature? Why to view
Would you, thus cruelly thofe fcenes unfold,
Which without pain and horror to behold,
Muft either fpeak me more or lefs than man;
Which friends may pardon, but I never can†.

" Having thus reciprocally rhapfodized, we difparted. The bard retired behind the umbrageous hedge, finally to accomplifh his interrupted repercuffions of communicated pleafures‡. As for myfelf, I was compelled to ambulate to Highgate, in order to evaporate the humidity of my habiliments, and contemper the malignity of frigorifick

---

* This rant of inimitable nonfenfe, contained in the above three paragraphs, is taken word for word from a celebrated modern. Vid. *Centaur not fabulous*.

† Vid. *Churchill's Conference*.

‡ Ramb. No. 148.

gorifick torpor with culinary irradiations.
The Caravanſeray to which my erratick ſteps
were accidentally conducted, was the em-
blematical ſign of fecundity and conſe-
quential cuckoldom at Highgate.    There,
according to the wonted modes and forma-
lities of the manſion I became obligated by
a double ſacramental ſtipulation : in the firſt
place, never to imbibe ſmall beer, whilſt I
could acquire convivial ale, unleſs the former were endued with higher powers of
ſenſitive gratification.    In the next place,
never to ſolicit an erratick gratification from
the menial fair, if I could obtain a reciprocation of delight * with the miſtreſs, unleſs
I believed the hand-maid poſſeſſed of greater
powers to kindle the ardour of enterprize,
ſet difficulties at defiance, ſtimulate perſe-
verance, and prevent the remiſſion of vi-
vour, when ſtanding in procinctu, on the
point of obtaining the recompence†.

    " The ceremonial perplexities attending
the conjuration, being finally adjuſted, I
entered into converſe with an Hibernian of
ſignal erudition, who ſate tranquilly puffing
the fumigations of his Calumet in an angle
of

* Ramb. 101.    † Ramb. No. 207.

of the fuliginous hexagonal apartment.
While we were univerfally engaged in the
vivacious loquacity of our evening compotations, he requefted me to ejaculate a fentimental effufion.   I bibulated * the falubrity
of our moft amiable fovereign,  the fafe par-
turition of his tranfcendental confort, and the
happy encreafe of the fons and daughters of
Britannick royalty †.   With difficulty my
learned friend repreffed his rifible powers at
this complicated fimplicity of my fentimental lore.  But he dignified my unimportance,
and corrected my inaccuracies ‡.   For when
it came to his turn, he effufed the moft
venerable and refpectable monofyllable, the
American belligerant, the fedulous domef-
tick damfel, the lamb-refembling fair one,
the Book-binder's confort, and the Mendi-
cant's benediction.

  " But the perfpicacity of my intellectual
powers, grafped not by intuition the recon-
dite fenfe of thofe fentimental allegories.
                                    Wonder

  * A cant word of the fame fort is put in Lexiphanes's mouth, by Lucian, on much the fame occafion.  See his Lexiphanes.   I muft own, however,
that I do not remember my hero has ufed it.

  † Raffelas, Vol. 1. p. 2.

  ‡ Ram. No. 139.

Wonder is a paufe of reafon, a fudden cef-
fation of the mental progrefs. I difentan-
gled not complications, nor invigorated my
confidence by conquefts over difficulty, but
flept in the gloomy acquiefcence of aftonifh-
ment, without efforts to animate enquiry,
or difpel obfcurity. Therefore I contented
myfelf with the gaze of folly, and refigned
the pleafure of rational contemplation to
more pertinatious ftudy, and more active
faculties †. For all my fcientifical acquifi-
tions are at laft concatenated into arguments
or compacted into fyftems, and nothing
henceforth can be to me fo odious as oppo-
fition, fo infolent as doubt, or fo dangerous
as novelty ‡.

In the fequel of our evening compotations, the fentimental Hibernian, with a
torpid refibility, fpontaneity of production,
and inflation of fpirit, burfting into abfurdity §, exhibited a variety of other allegories,
infinitely more complicated than the former,
but

† Ram. No. 137.
‡ Ram. No. 151. I am inclined to believe, that
in this fentence, Lexiphanes has unknowingly
drawn his own character.
§ Ramb. No. 124, 131, 195.

but of all which he gave fuch explications, that he raifed the eafy facetioufnefs and flowing hilarity of our fellow compotators to the higheſt pinnacle of exaltation. Burſts of merriment, and flaſhes of tranfport broke forth like corufcations of lightening, and we difturbed the neighbourhood with the vociferations of our applaufe.

" As we had now attained the fublimeſt pinnacle of merriment, it was all of a fudden intercepted *, our gaiety darkened, and a totality of confufion introduced by the exhibition of a violent altercation between a Grocer of fignal celebrity, corpulency, and opulency in Cheapfide, and a raw-bon'd, hard-faced, high-cheeked Caledonian, who had arrived thus far in his erratick progrefs from his native barren heaths, tò the fertilized meadows circumjacent about this metropolis, in the inveſtigation of preferment. We were all holding our fides, totally convulfed with univerfal laughter, when the Grocer emitted a thundering roar of poſterior vociferation. The convivial affociates were ſtartled as at the fudden and unexpected

ex-

* Raffelas.

explofion of ordinance; and the Caledonian. fcratching his head, and appall'd gazing the corpulent prefence * over his left fhoulder, addreffed him thus in the vulgar dialect of his provincial barbarifm. Are thae the manners of you braw London fôk ? giff it be fae, I wifs 1 was e'en at my ain hame agen. The Grocer vouchfafed not a reply, manifefted not the leaft fignal of villatick bafhfulnefs, but elevating his left leg with all the compofure of calm deliberation, ex-hibited a fecond vociferation, louder and more fonorous than the former. At the fame time, though it had neither efcaped our auditory, nor our olfactory nerves, he clenched his fift, gave the bench before him a collifion, eyed the Caledonian with an emphatical fignificance of gaze, and be-ing a true-born Englifhman, as well as a fignal patriot cried out, with a blaft of e-ructation, *Lord B----* . The Caledonian became now the object of undiftinguifh-ed merriment. The fierce illapfe of paf-fion rouzed the whole fabrick of his mind,

* Appall'd, I gaz'd, the godlike prefence. Pleaf. of Imagination, B. 2. L. 23.

mind *, and his native ferocity being highly exacerbated; he vented not his wrath in
a reciprocation of reproaches, but having
inftantaneous recurrence to fiftical ratiocination beftowed a violent percuffion on the
corpulent Grocer's nafal promontory, which,
in a moment, fuffufed with fanguinary
ftreams, his plenilunar refplendent countenance, and tarnifhed gold laced waiftcoat.

" Ferocious inftillations of difcord were
now transfufed by a rapid diffemination
through the bofoms of the convivial and hitherto pacifick compotators. The Grocer
debilitated by the imbecillity and decrepitude of age, and the exercitation of his priftine bruifing powers having been long reftrained by the unwieldinefs of corpulency,
fuccumbed under the furies of force with
the liftleffnefs of languor and defpondency
of inferiority. But a Foe to Cattle, tho' a
friend to the Grocer, and of equal celebrity
for patriotick principles and liberal exhibition of pofterior vociferation, challenged
and attacked the two-legged Confumer of
Oats. Nor wanted either Butcher or Confumer, Friends Allies and Confederates.

D                              The

* Pleafures of Imagination.

The former was affifted by the auxiliar virtues and fubfidiary aids of patriots, anterior
eru{ctators, and pofterior vociferators; and
the latter by courtiers, his fellow-confumers
of Oats, and joint muficians on the Caledonian violoncello. Entirely inefficacious and
totally fruftraneous were all the mediatory
interceffions and reconciliatory interpofi-
tions of myfelf, and the fentimental Hibernian, for a fufpenfion of hoftilities, and a general pacification. Finding the hearts of
the antagonifts irremediably exacerbated
with the corrofion of hatred, and reciprocation of mifchief and reproaches, we concluded to repofe in the fhades of neutrality,
and avoid a fortuitous percuffion under the
fhelter of diftance.

" Thus a combat royal enfued, a circulatory war commenced. Various were the
changes, viciffitudes and perplexities from
the mutability of fortune, and victory long
hung doubtful in the trepidations of the balance and fluctuations of uncertainty. At
laft, by the fortuitous fupervention and
·fpontaneous intervention of the bard, in whom
conftellated * with equal luftre all bruifing
and poetical powers, who fatiated of his
fufceptible

* Rambler, No. 201.

fufceptible nymph, had juft made a re-linquifhment, the patriotick fifts became preponderant. And now had a total dif-comfiture of the rifible Oat-confumers en-fued, had not the Caledonian who began the civil difcord, and inteftine conflagration, alarmed two Highland militants then quar-tered in the Caravanferay by his idiomatical vociferation. Is there nae help here for poor Scotland ? bauled he out with reiterated ef-forts. At laft the variegated militants ap-peared, making flaming circulatory irradi-ations with their brandifhed broad fwords, and emitting terrible facramental denounci-ations of mortal purpofe, of inftant ven-geance, death and deftruction. The com-batants immediately furceafed, and the Gro-cer, all terror-ftruck with the dreadful ex-hibition, occumbed in a fwoon. Our olfac-tory powers were now overcome by the o-doriferous fteams that iffued from him in a moft exuberant effufion, and afforded us a conjectural glimpfe of what had been tranf-acted under his femoral habiliments. A par-ley then enfued between the Murtherer of Bullocks and Confumer of Oats, and preli-minary articles for an amicable congrefs were finally adjufted. The Foe to Cattle obtefted

that

that he entertained no antipathy to the Caledonian emigrant or his country; and the
two-legged Confumer of Oats deprecated his
forgivenefs for affaulting his convivial affociate the Grocer, and above all, for infringing
the *Claim of Rights*, the *Magna Charta* of all
true-born Englifhmen, with refpect to the liberal publick and unreftrained exhibition of
their powers of anterior eructation and pofterior vociferation; and promifed with all the
folemnity of ftipulation, that he would never
offend in a point of that tender and delicate
concernment for the future.

" Thus a perfect harmony, and a general tranquillity were happily reftored. And
a lafting and permanent pacification, of
which the learned Hibernian and myfelf had
been the mediators, and were now the Gua-
rantees, was finally concluded, on terms, by
which the refpective honours and interefts
of the belligerent powers were equally confulted. A reciprocal and moft amicable
intermixture and conquaffation of hands,
with the moft refpectful profeffions in the
moft fonorous periods of everlafting amity,
paft now between the Cow-killer and Oat-
meal-eater. They vociferated for fupernumerary

merary pots of porter, with all the ardour
of impatience, which were introduced and
evacuated with all the filent·celerity of time.
Finally, of this civil commotion, this national diffention, no confequential traces re-
mained, but excremental effufions in the
Grocer's femoral habiliments, cerulean fanguinary fuffufious all around the Caledonian's luminaries, and a pruriginous, herpeti-
cal and incurable eruption of puftules in the
digitary interftices, and over the brachial
regions which the murtherer of bullocks
had contracted by a too frequent, prolong-
ed and intimate contact with the correfpond-
ing members of his novel confederate and
convivial affociate, the two-leggedConfumer
of Oats *.

* It is faid, foreign gentlemen are at prefent much
addicted to the ftudy of our language. A thing I
am heartily forry fhould take place, till the tafte of
the publick, at leaft, with refpect to the authors we
admire, be a little amended. They may not only
entertain a very contemptible opinion of us as to
that article, but alfo be led to conceive the ftrangeft
notions of our laws, cuftoms and manners; and
what is yet more unlucky, conclude, that the natives of one of our three kingdoms are really no
better than irrational, irrifible, four-legged ani-
mals, and confidered by their fellow-fubjects, and

the

" The fentimental Hibernian, and myfelf, left them in the height of their amicable com- potations and fimultaneoufly returned to

the legiflature in no other capacity. I am led into this train of reflection, by the following advertife- ment, which I met with the other day in the Daily Advertifer.

" The confumers of oats, within the cities of Lon- don and Weftminfter, and Borough of Southwark, and who fubfcribed towards the expences of obtain- ing the laft act of parliament for empowering the juftices in London to grant a certificate of the price of oats, four times a year, are defired to meet their Committee, at the Sun-Tavern, in St. Paul's Church- yard, this day, being the 19th of December inftant, at five o'clock in the afternoon, on fpecial af- fairs."

Now, whoever confiders the definition of oats, given by Lexiphanes in his dictionary, and quoted in page 23d of this dialogue, cannot conceive any thing to be meant by *Confumers of Oats*, in the ge- neral and comprehenfive fenfe of the expreffion, o- ther than *English horfes or mares*, and *Scotch men or women*. 'Tis certain, a foreigner who ftudies our language grammatically, and who muft naturally look upon this work of our renown'd Lexicographer, as the ftandard of our tongue, and have recourfe to it, in order to learn the ftrength and idiom, and peculiar meaning and energy of our words and phra- fes ; 'tis certain, I fay, that fuch a perfon, in fuch a cafe, could underftand nothing elfe by it. What then

Gray's-Inn, in the periodical itinerant vehicle.
And there I had not long been, when Mega-
lonymus, the Attorney, inchoated an action

then muſt he think of the above advertiſement?
will he not naturally conclude, that 'tis an ordinary thing in London, for Horſes and Scotch men to
meet at a tavern, like friends and acquaintances,
over a bottle ; to appoint committees, out of their
reſpective bodies, to conſult together on their ſpe-
cial affairs ; and jointly to addreſs ſuch a venerable
ſociety as their worſhips, the Juſtices, about their
neareſt and moſt important concern, namely, the
*price of Oats, their common food.*
Ambiguities of this kind, which may be produc-
tive of very troubleſome miſtakes and inconvenien-
cies, are great imperfections in a language, and
ought carefully to be guarded againſt. It would
be labour thrown away to petition the great Lexiphanes, to alter one tittle, or jôta of his dictionary,
and to accommodate it to our weakneſs and prejudices ; barely to ſuggeſt the expediency of ſuch a meaſure, would be high treaſon againſt his *Lexicogra-
phical powers* and authority. I muſt therefore content myſelf with beſeeching the ingenious compilers
of the Daily Advertiſer, the next time they have
occaſion to inſert ſuch an advertiſement, that they
would have the goodneſs to add, to *Conſumers of Oats,*
the epithets of *Two-legged Riſible* or *Rational.* Yet,
on ſecond thoughts, even this honourable addition
will not altogether do the buſineſs. For as I hum-
bly apprehend no Engliſhman, can be ſaid, in the
proper

against me, at the suit of the mercenary own-
er of the conductitious palfrey, which, in the
courfe

proper and obvious fenfe, to be a confumer of oats.
No, they are confumers of the whiteft of wheat-
flour, adulterated only with lime and allum, and
fome few other poifonous materials. That, however, is nothing. Therefore in the room of *Confumers*, I would haveThem fubftitute *Buyers* and *Sellers*,
which will effectually anfwer the purpofe.

The advice I have given, I have myfelf followed.
For wherever the Caledonian, the hero in the national quarrel occafioned by that *true-born Englifhman* and *fignal patriot the Grocer*, is mentioned as a
*Confumer of Oats*, I have conftantly added the diftinction of Two-legged or *Rifible*, that he might at
no time be miftaken for a Horfe, his brother *Confumer*. But I have not ventured to honour him with
the addition of rational, as apprehending the whole
being put in Lexiphanes's mouth, that might be out
of character. For he is known to hold the northern
inhabitants of our ifland in fuch fovereign contempt,
that it is much to be queftioned whether he reckons
them an order of beings fuperior to Bears or Ba-
boons. However Their property of two-leggednefs
can never be difputed, and I hope many of them
have fhewn their *Powers* of *Rifibility*, by laughing
very heartily at Him. For in fact, I know not a
more laughable, a more ridiculous object in the
univerfe, than fuch a folemn, felf-conceited, haughty,
over-bearing, pedantick old-fchool-boy, as my
Lexiphanes.

courfe of his vertiginous gambols, had taken an erratick progrefs to fuch a diftance,
and with fuch velocity, that he could not
be re-apprehended. The bard confcious that
the violence of his repercuffions, and the im-
petuofity*of his impaffioned nerve, was the
priftine caufe of all my complicated infelicities,
and comick calamities §, has procured me the
furety of his two bookfellers. My council is
Pertinax†, who being early initiated in a thoufand low ftratagems, nimble fhifts, and fly
concealments, contracted an intellectual malady which infected his reafon, and from
blafting the bloffoms of knowledge, pro-
ceeded in time to canker its root. At riper
years, he caught the contagion of vanity,
and diftinguifhed himfelf by fophifms and
paradoxes till his ideas were confufed, his
judgment embaraffed, and his intellects diftorted. But growing weary of a perpetual
equipoife of the mind, he prefcribed a new
regimen to his underftanding, and being at
length recovered from his argumental delirium, with which he was wont to darken
gaiety,

* This word is mightily commended for fonñd,
&c. in the Elem. of Criticifm.    § Ramb. No. 176.
† See Pertinax's Letter, No. 95.

gaiety, and perplex ratiocination, he now applies his powers with great sedulity to the acquirement of legiflative fcience. The the trial makes its approximation with the filent celerity of time, notwithftanding

The laws delay, the proud man's contumely,
The infolence of office, and the fpurns
Which patient merit of th' unworthy takes.

" I had no fooner effufed this ejaculation to Hypertatus, than Mifocapelus, Herme-ticus, Hymeneus, Captator, Eubulus, and Quifquilius || came up and * conjoined us. It was impoffible for me not to fuccumb § un-der the conjunct importunities of fo many illuftrious affociates, who all fimultaneoufly‡ obfecrated me to accompany them in an ambulatory project to the wakeful harbinger of day ** at Chelfea, and there to recreate and invigorate our powers with buns, con-vivial ale, and a fober erratick game at fkittles. At length I adhibited my confent, though with an extremity of reluctance, owing to the implacability of the pain of my fundamental excoriations, which were
fo

---

, || Characters or correfpondents of our Author in the Rambler.
* Elements of Criticifm. § Robertfon. ‡ Hume.
** In Englifh the fign of the Cock.

fo highly exafperated by the adhefions of my everlafting thickfets, that defpair grafp- ed my agonizing bofom, and I dreaded their termination in a fiftula. But the pleafing powers † and grateful honours of their con- verfation, and above all, converting my thoughts to the ambition of aerial crowns,

And fuperlunary felicities, ‡

obtunded the acrimony of my dolorous fituation.

" Mifocapelus § had paffed his officinal ftate behind the counter of a haberdafher; he had applied all his powers to the know- ledge of his trade, fo that he quickly be- came a critick in fmall wares, and a fkilfull contriver of new mixtures of colorifick vari- ety. In the fourth year of his officinalfhip he paid a vifit to his rural friends, where he expected to be confulted as a mafter of pecu- niary knowledge, and oracle of the mode. But, unhappily, a colonel of the guards, with a carelefs gaiety and unceremonious civility; and a ftudent of the Temple, w.th lefs attraction of mien, but greate powers

of

---

† Akenfide.    ‡ Night T    
§ See Mifocapelus's Letters,

of elocution, fo abftracted all his auditors
whilft he was exhaufting his defcriptive powers in a minute reprefentation of a lord
mayor's triumphal folemnity, that thence-
forth he could exhibit no other proofs of
his exiftence, than naming the toaft in his
turn. After the death of his elder brother,
who died of drunken joy, he commenced
gentleman, but with great infelicity of attempt. For with a double quantity of lace
on his coat, a forbidding frown, a fmile of
condefcenfion, a flight falutation, an abrupt
departure, and a vertiginous motion on his
heel with much levity and fprightlinefs, he
has not attained his refolution of dazzling
intimacy to a fitter diftance, or inhibiting
its approaches with its ufual phrafes of benevolence. He has had fucceffive circum-
rotations through the characters of Squire,
Critick, Gamefter, and Foxhunter, but has
at laft degenerated into that of a Taylor;
in which capacity he has been recommended
to all her numerous circle of acquaintance,
by the mifchievous generofity of Ferocula,
whom he once affifted, in the prefence of
hundreds, in an altercation for fix-pence
with a hackney coachman.

" Hymenæus

" § Hymenæus, a curious indagator * into feminine fecrets, had long been an unfuccefsful hymeneal folicitor, and feemed to lie under the penal feverity of being doomed to frozen celibacy, and of being excluded by an irreverfible decree from all hopes of connubial felicity. He breathed out the fighs of his firft affection at the feet of the gay, the fparkling, the vivacious Ferocula, for he looked with veneration on her readinefs of expedients, contempt of difficulty, affurance of addrefs, and promptitude of reply†. He paid his fubfequent addreffes to the deep-read Mifothea, the inexorable enemy of ignorant pertnefs and puerile levity, who fcarcely condefcended to infufe tea but for the linguift, the geometrician, the aftronomer, or the poet. She was only to be gained by the fcholar who could overpower her by difputation. Amidft the fondeft ardours of courtfhip fbe could call for a definition, and contemned every argument for fixing the day of his felicity, that could not be reduced

§ For the hard words and Lexiphanick beauties of this paragraph, confult the letters figned Hymenæus and Tranquilla, in the Rambler.

* Night Thoughts † A Quaternion.

duced to regular fyllogiftical argumentation.
.Thirdly, he folicited connubial conjunction
with the calm, the prudent, the oeconomical Sophronia, but furely it might be for-
given him if he forgot the decency of common forms, when from an excefs of her
oeconomical folicitudes * fhe difcharged her
maid Phillida for breaking fix teeth of an
ivory comb, which had coft her three half
crowns. Soon after, an invitation to fup
with one of his bufy hymeneal folicitors,
made him, by a concerred chance, acquainted with Camilla. He could not fupprefs
fome raptures of admiration and flutters of
defire, and was eafily perfuaded to make
nearer approximations. But he found that
fhe made fuch generous advances to the
verges of virility, that he thought not his
quiet and honour to be entrufted to fuch au-
dacious virtue, which could not but be
fugacious †, as it was hourly courting danger, and foliciting affault. His next miftrefs was the nicely tricked Nitella, but he
was difgufted at the fuperftitious regularity
of her apartments, the occafionality and
ambitioufnefs

* Rambler, No. 162.
† Sterne's Sermons.

ambitioufnefs of her drefs, and want of familiarization to her own ornaments. And now his evil deftiny conducted him to Charybdis, whofe moderate defires for feals and fnuff-boxes, rifing by degrees to a rapacity for gold and diamonds, effectuated a fuperaddition of one more, to fix and forty fruftraneous hymeneal folicitors. Laftly, Imperia took poffeffion of his heart, bnt kept it not long. He left her to grow wife at leifure, or continue in errour at her own expence. Thus he had hitherto paffed his life in frozen celibacy. His friends indeed told him, that he dreffed up an ideal charmer in all the radiance of perfection, and then entered the world to gaze for a fimilar excellency in corporeal beauty. But furely it was not madnefs to hope for fome terreftrial lady unftained. At laft, through the intervention of the Rambler, and without any danger of malignant fafcination, or multiplying ftipulations, he was coalited * in a connubial conjunction with Tranquilla, whofe ears had been made delicate by riot of adulation †, who had danced the round of gaiety amidft the murmurs of envy and gratulations

* Hume's Hiftory.
† Rambler, No. 119.

gratulations of applaufe, been attended from pleafure to pleafure by the fuperciliufnefs of grandeur, the levity of fprightlinefs, and the glitter of vanity*; and feen her regard folicited by the obfequioufnefs of gallantry, the gaiety of wit, and timidity of love §. Their profpects were fuch, that they fpread themfelves into the boundlefs regions of eternity. But they were doomed to give one inftance more of the uncertainty of human difcernment, and the fragility of connubial hopes of felicity. The extreme delicacy of Tranquilla had been fomewhat offended at a warty excrefcence on the tip of Hymeneus's little finger; and that of Hymeneus in totality difgufted at a fmall mole obumbrated with a cerulean exuberance of capillary honours on the infide of Tranquilla's femoral regions, a little above the dexter genuflexion. They now became diffocial, and their children were foris-famaliated. And Hymeneus unable to reprefs the accumulated invigoration of his powers, has grown enamoured of the generick † habit, and interdicted happinefs of incidental repercuffions,

---

* Rambler, No. 145.    § A double Triad.
† Elements of Criticifm.

repercuffions, in the felection of which he is determined by the vibratiuncles and armature of Hermeticus's artificial magnets.

Hermeticus has for a long time applied his corporeal and mental powers to the wonders every day produced by the pokers of magnetifm and wheels of electricity. He has fallen eleven times fpeechlefs with electrical fhocks, he has twice diflocated his limbs, and once fractured his fkull in effaying to fly, and four times endangered his life by fubmitting to the transfufion of blood. But he has now entered into a zealous competition for magnetical fame. Owing to a hint of the Rabbi Abraham ben Hannafe, he has difcovered a method of detecting connubial wickednefs, and preferving the connubial compact from violation. It is an armature of a particular metallick compofition, which concentrates the virtue, and determines the agency of magnets, to difcover, by the nature and quality of their reciprocating vibratiuncles, all the different modifications wherein breaches of connubial fidelity and the laws of chaftity had been confummated.

E " Eubulus

" Eubulus is now labouring in the wheel
of anxious dependance. His uncle, who
fupplied him with exuberance of money,
and maintained him in pecuniary impudence
that he might learn to become his dignity
when he fhould be made Lord Chancellor,
which he often lamented that the increafe
of his imbecillities and his decrepitude was
very likely to preclude him from feeing,
had frequently harraffed him with monitory
letters. But Eubulus at laft refolved to
teach young men in what manner grey-
bearded infolence ought to be treated. He
therefore, one evening, took his pen in
hand, and after having rouzed his powers
to a due ftate of animation with a catch,
wrote a general anfwer to all his monitions
with fuch vivacity of turn, fuch elegancy of
irony, and fuch afperity of farcafm, that he
convulfed a large company with univerfal
laughter, kindled up an undiftinguifhed
blaze of merriment, raifed an unintermitted
ftream of jocularity, difturbed the whole
neighbourhood with vociferations of ap-
applaufe, and five days afterwards was an-
fwered, that he muft be content to live upon
his own eftate.

Captator

" Captator had an unrefifting fupplenefs of temper, and an infatiable wifh for riches, yet he never felt the ftimulations of curio-fity, nor ardour of adventure.   Therefore, when the failor propofed a voyage, he fell fick under his mother's direction, who em-ployed fuch fuperfluity of artifice, that fhe was with difficulty perfuaded not to endan-ger her health with nocturnal attendance. This deceit was difcovered to the failor by his mother's handmaid, when he made her amo-rous advances, and folicited her with hyme-neal ftipulations.   The Squire was likewife difgufted, and he now depends folely on the Chambermaid ; and if the old woman fhould likewife at laft deceive him, is in danger at once of beggary and ignorance.

" Quifquilius has brought inconvenien-cies on  himfelf by  an  unextinguifhable ar-dour of curiofity, and an unremitted per-feverance in the acquifition of the produc-tions of art and nature.   Yet he does not wifh to ftimulate the envy of unfuccefsful collectors by too pompous a difplay of his fcientifick wealth.    Thefe accumulations have not been made without fome diminu-tion of his fortune ; he has transferred his money from the funds to his clofet, and has at laft mortgaged his land, to purchafe thirty medals which he could never find before. For curiofity trafficking with avarice, the wealth of India had not been enough. The cruelty of his creditors has made an expilation of his repofitory, and he will be conftrained to diffeminate, by a rapid fale, what the labour of an age will not re-collect and re-affemble. He has made me a prefent of two vials, in one of which is dew brufhed from a Banana, in the gardens of Ifpahan; in the other brine, that once vertiginated in the pacifick ocean, for which he defires no other recompence, than that I fhould recommend his catalogue to the publick.

" Such were my convivial affociates +? and while we continued our viatorial progreffion through the royal perambulations we fortuitoufly occurred that celeftial meditant Mr. James Hervey, in whom exuberance of mag-. nanimous fentiment and ebullition of genius * are fo fignally conftellated. Our occurrence was near the gate heretofore denominated from a nobleman on whofe producti-

ons

+ For thefe four characters, fee Ramb. No. 199, 26, 198, 82.          * Ramb. No. 129.

ons there is no ſtamp of genius *, but which are in reality pages of inanity. But it is now, with greater propriety of appellation, dignified from our moſt amiable ſovereign's tranſcendental conſort. Without pre-ſuppoſing impoſſibilities or anticipating fruſtration, we ſolicited his company with the ſonorous † periods of refpectful profeſſion, that while we ſhould be diſporting with the bowl and pins, he might be agglomerating meditations on the penſile ſpiky pods of the blooming religioſos of the gardens ; but he tranſmitted us a declinature in the monoſyllables of coldneſs, for he was going to effuſe the fair creation ‡ of his praying

E 3                     powers

* Sheffield, Duke of Buckingham. This is the character given by Warton, in his Eſſay on Pope, of that Nobleman's writings. I own that Lexiphanes does not, in ſo many words, call them pages of *Inanity.* He applies that expreſſion to Walſh. But he does what is equivalent. He ſays, in his Idler, I think, poſterity will wonder how ſuch men as Sheffield and Lanſdowne ever came to have any reputation. What muſt poſterity think of the preſent age in which this dogmatical pedant has ob-. tained ſo great a reputation !

† Ramb. No. 194.

‡ Pleaſ. of Imag. B. 2. L. 38.

powers at the bed-fide of a penitential nymph in Lewkener's lane. However, he gave us a promiffory note he would fubjoin a defcant on the creation *.

" At length we arrived at the place of our original deftination, without any inter-cepting † interruption; only Hymenæus and Hermeticus would have diverted into the fountain in the Five Fields, in order to try fome magnetical experiments on an ambu-latory nymph, who feemed perpetually fuf-ceptible of occafional delight. But they were reftrained, as well by the unexpected appearance of Tranquilla, who juft then tollutated along in a rotatory vehicle, as by the unanimous fimultaneity of our prohibi-tory fupplications. On our ingrefs into the fcene of fkittleary contention, we expedited ambaffadors with plenary powers to procure us buttered buns, charming Chefhire cheefe, tart tit-bit tartlets, rare ripe radifhes, and recent rolls ‡; we enhanced our reciprocal felicity by quaffing convivial Burton; and

---

* Hervey's Meditations.          † Raffelas.

‡ Alliteration; a figure Lexiphanes feems to be fometimes very fond of, though I do not fay he has evercarried it to that excefs of affectation, in which it

is

we difported with the bowl and pins. At laft, after various viciffitudes and revolutions of a vehement contention, and ardent competition for fkittleary reputation, the totality of the reckoning devolved upon Quifquilius. Quifquilius, being devoid of pecuniary ftores, offered to depofite as a mode of hypothecal fecurity, the ftings of four wafps, that had been taken torpid in their winter quarters. But the landlord rejected the proffer with an indignant fneer of pecuniary impudence. Quifquilius vainly alledged, with all the powers of deprecating rhetorical perfuafion, that the wafps from whom the ftings had been extracted, coft him the annual rent of the farm where they had been caught, when under the influence of frigorifick torpor. The unfeeling governor of the caravanferay replied not, but with a trite faying of proverbial vulgarifm. A fool and his money are foon parted. At laft, after a tedious altercation,

E 4 Mifo-

---

is found in the paffage referred to, or in the foregoing *favory fheeps-heads*, *prime pigs pettytoes*, and *plump plumb-pudding*; but I thought it not amifs, to give into the *Caricatura* a little now and then, a thing I have feldom had occafion of doing.

Mifocapelus, inftigated by the ramifications of private friendfhip, difburfed the fymbol.

"When now we had with fome difficulty effectuated a relinquifhment of this dignified fcene of fkittleary contention, a dufky and cerulean darknefs had begun to obumbrate the fuperficies of the conftellated regions, and to diminifh the horizon of our profpects. We ambulated homeward, aided by the declining corufcations of a crepufcular glimmering. In our viatorial progreffion, we were now oppofite the Portobello, where latrocinary Homicides wont to lurk, and make incurfions on unfufpecting way-farers, and comminutions of their purfes and lives. Terrification feized me from the drearinefs of the fcene, and the reflection that the ghofts of the murdered might now be hovering round the fatal places where their terreftrial exiftences had been comminuted. Eubulus, that infidel and infolent contemner of grey-bearded wifdom, obferving the tremulous commotion of my nerves, and entertaining a conjectural glimpfe of my mental fituation, apprehended me by the fleeve, vociferating with all the femblance of terror: Behold an apparition,

tion, the ghoft of a murdered traveller! I adverted my luminaries directly forward, and gazed an object feemingly of immenfe magnitude, and arrayed in a vefture of fhining radiance. I fuffered a reduplication of horrifick terrors, and again Eubulus exclaimed. Tis FANNY! tis Mifs FANNY herfelf, the very identical ghoft of Cock-lane! fhe is come to punifh and terrify a fceptical unbelieving world. Heareft thou not, her percuffions of negation, her repercuffions of affirmation, and her fcalpations of indignation *!

" Succumbing now under an accumulation of horrors, actuated as if I had been a meer involuntary mechanift, and having inter-

---

* It feems, that in the language of the famous Cock-lane Ghoft, a fingle knock fignified *No*, a double one *Yes*, and fcratching imported *difpleafure*. Tis pity *Mifs Fanny* fo foon difcontinued her vifits to this world, otherwife, it may be prefumed, Lexiphanes, who, 'tis faid, was a very diligent and attentive fcholar, would have become as great an adept in the dialect of Ghofts, as Homer was in that of the Gods, or as he is himfelf in his own mother tongue. It might, in time, have furnifhed our great Lexicographer with materials for a dictionary of the *Language of Spirits.*

interjected a circumftantial paufe †, I thus
ejaculated.

Angels and minifters of grace defend us !
Be thou a fpirit of health ! or goblin damn'd !
Bring with thee airs from heaven, or blafts from
      hell ! !
Be thy events wicked or charitable !
Thou com'ft in fuch a queftionable fhape
That I will fpeak to thee ! I'll call thee FANNY
Maid ! miftrefs ! injur'd fair ! what may this
      mean
That thou dead coarfe again, in winding fheet,
Revifit'ft thus the glimpfe crepufcular
Making it hideous ; and us FOOLS of NA-
      TURE
So horribly to fhake our difpofitions
With thoughts beyond the reaches of our fouls.
Wherefore, what may this mean ?

Whilft thus ejaculating, Hypertatus with
that magnanimity of fentiment, that un-
dauntednefs of refolution, and that intrepi-
dity of courage, derived from his habitation
in the elevated regions of a garret, approach-
ed the place where the apparition feemed to
lie, fixed in torpid immobility. But at his
approximation it ftarted like a guilty thing,
          and

† Elements of Criticifm.

and ran vagiffating along the Champain, as if it had been the youthful mafculine off-fpring of a Tauro-vaccineal conjunction.

" At this unexpected exhibition, my fel-low compotators were totally convulfed with univerfal laughter; and even Hypertatus himfelf, my moft amicable convivial affo-ciate, could not altogether reprefs the in-ftantaneous motions of merriment *. As for myfelf, I reprehended Eubulus, with the fonorous vociferations of anger, and told him that the precipitation of his inex-perience ought to be fhackled by a proper timidity +; and that though he had anfwer-ed his uncle's monitory letters with fuch vi-vacity of turn, fuch elegancy of irony, and fuch afperity of farcafm, that he had left him henceforth to live upon his own eftate; and that though he had retorted the irony of his patron Hilarius, equally renowned for the extent of his knowledge, the elegance of his diction, and the acutenefs of his wit with fuch fpirit, that he foon convinced him his purpofe was not to encourage a rival, but

* Ramb. No. 176.
+ Ramb. No. 159.

but to fofter a parafite *; I told him, I fay,
that he fhould not with impunity derogate
from my dictatorial importance, remuneratory
honours, and accumulations of preparatory
knowledge, with the pertnefs of puerility,
the levity of contempt, and the derifion of
ridicule. Eubulus, though he could hardly articulate for a fuffocation of rifibility,
declared with facramental obteftations, that
he had himfelf laboured under fimilar powers of deception. I believed him not, and
threatened to convict him of the tortuofity
of his imaginary rectitude by manual fyllo-
gifms, fiftical applications, and baculinary
argumentation.

" But Hypertatus recalled us from ex-
centricity †, and by an extemporaneous
fprightlinefs, a happy interruption, and antidotal intervention, repreffed our animofi-
ty, compofed our differences, and reftored
our Hilarity. He lured and rouzed us from
a vivacious loquacity, a torpid rifibility,
and languifhment of inattention ‡, by effu-
fing, in a ftrain of peculiar eloquence, an
elaborate differtation on the multiplicity of
bufinefs,

---

* Ramb. No. 26, 27.    † Ramb. No. 151.
‡ Ramb. No. 124.

bufinefs, aftonifhing intellectual powers, and accelerated train of perceptions § in the mind of the dwarfifh drawer, Mr. John Coan. It is not to be conceived, faid he, what length a habit of activity in affairs will carry fome men. Let a ftranger, or let any per-fon to whom the fight is not familiar, attend the drawer at the Cock, through the labours but of one day, during a feafon of fkittle-playing: How great will be his aftonifh-ment! What multiplicity of in-and-out-of-doors-bufinefs, what profound attention, and what elaborate application to matters of Beer-drawing! The train of perceptions muft, in this great diminutive, be accele-rated far beyond the common courfe of na-ture. Yet no confufion nor hurry; but in every reckoning the greateft juftnefs and ac-curacy. Such is the force of habit! How happy is man to have the command of a principle of action, that can elevate him fo

far

§ The rhapfody drawing now near a clofe, I have *exhaufted* all my *powers*, in bringing together, in this and the two foregoing paragraphs, a ftring of Mr. J———'s favourite figures of fpeech, namely, of fenfelefs unmeaning *Triads*, all in the true Lexi-phanick tafte, and moft of 'em really to be found in his Ramblers.

far above the ordinary condition of humanity ! *

" On our ingreding the royal walks we
became diffocial and difparted. Mifoca-
capelus, Captator, Eubulus, and Quifquilius properated before, with a rapid ofci-

* This rant of Hypertatus, only reading *Chancellor of Great Britain*, for *Drawer at the Cock*, *law-bufi-
nefs* for *in-and-out-of-doors-bufinefs*, *feffion of Parliament*,
for *feafon of Skittle-playing*, and *government*, for *beer-
drawing*, is almoft word for word a rant in the
Elements of Criticifm, in praife of a late Chancellor.
The original was compofed, as the margin informs
us, in 1753, the parody in 1763. The reader may
confult what the fame author fays a few pages afterwards, about ridicule and parodies. He juftly ob-
ferves, that a parody may be fuccefsfully ufed either
when it does or does not ridicule the original paffage
it refers to. The foregoing is a parody of the former
fort. For, as it happens, the thoughts, fuch as they
are, may be applied with the fame truth and propriety to either perfonage, whether the Chancellor
or the Drawer, provided they be alike expert in their
refpective occupations. And it likewife affordeth
us, a very apt and happy inftance to fhew how much
ridicule is the teft of truth and juftnefs of thought;
which by the by this very ingenious writer proveth
in the chapter referred to, and in a clearer and con-
cifer manner than I remember to have met with.
The reafon is what follows. Lord K —— confines
the praifes of a very great man, I believe, to qualities,

                                                    fuch

tancy. The Squire to his firſt floor, the reſt to their garrets. I lingered behind, detained by my fundamental malady. Hymenæus, Hermeticus, and Hypertatus preſerved a ſimilar pace, curious to gaze the venal charms of ambling nymphs. Amidſt the various conflux of ſuch peripateticks, Hymenæus had a fortuitous occurrence with Miſella. He accoſted the wandering fair,

he

---

ſuch as meer habits, a quick ſucceſſion of perceptions and tranſition from one ſort of buſineſs to another, qualities that are common and in equal or greater perfection among the loweſt vulgar, and employed by them in the meaneſt and moſt inſignificant purſuits. Whereas had he celebrated him for the difficulty and importance of his acquirements, his inflexible integrity and unceaſing labours in the ſervice of his country and in the duties of his high and exalted office, I think in that caſe the keeneſt and moſt licentious ridicule might be ſafely ſet at defiance, provided however there were no quaint affected or Lexiphanick expreſſions, ſuch as the *retarded* or *accelerated train of perceptions*, &c. This reflection appears to me ſo obvious, I wonder it eſcaped the author, eſpecially one who hath ſkewn ſuch depth of thought and admirable penetration in unfolding the moſt intricate turnings and windings of the human heart, underſtanding and conſtitution.

he fimulated * a paffion for her, and invited her to Haddock's. Hymenæus, Herme-ticus and Mifella, entered boldly at the ever-open gate. But Hypertatus and myfelf ob-ferved fome very refpectable bookfellers en-gaged in an ambulatory project under the piazza's vault. Thofe worthies, who, ac-cording to a dignified author of fignal cele-brity for critical and paradoxical powers, † are even in this enlightened age, neither the worft judges nor the leaft rewarders of literary merit ‡, had engaged Hypertatus, with vehement injunctions of hafte, to write a full and candid confutation of all the falfe reafonings, abfurd mifreprefentation of facts, and infidious infinuations, contained in the laft political pamphlet, which, if we may truft the veracity of fame, was his own pro-duction; and they had me likewife under terms of ftrict obligation, to compofe a perpetual commentary on the immortal pro-

ductions

---

* The World. This is, perhaps, the only Lexi-phanick word in the elegant papers that go by that name.

† See W——n's preface to his edition of Shake-fpear.

‡ Witnefs the high price given for *Paradife Loft.*

duations of the divine Shakefpear\*; therefore, fearful of their collifion, and elufive
of their gaze, by a low ſtratagem, nimble
ſhift, and ſly concealment, we made our
entry at the poſtern gate in Hart-ſtreet. We
conjoined our aſſociates in an apartment
whence all the evils of life ſeemed extraſted
and excluded, and we heard the dance of
feſtivity, and the ſong of mirth. While
we were evacuating a goblet of mantling
arrack, Hermeticus made a magnetical ex-
periment on Mifella, which, though it was
performed with a magnet of the moſt ſlug-
giſh and inert ſpecies, difcovered that during
the laſt diurnal circumrotation, ſhe had re-
ciprocated civilities with four and twenty
different afcenfors. Mifella retired to an ad-
joining apartment, whither Hymenæus ſoon
followed her. But in the mean time he
defcanted very philofophically, and effuſed
many ſage reflections on the fugacioufneſs
of connubial felicity, and inſtability of human enjoyments. On making his exit, he

F                              ap-

---

\* When this was written, Mr. J———'s edition of
Shakefpear was only in expeſtancy. It hath ſince been
publiſhed, and even in the judgment of the public,
ſo much prejudiced in his favour, has fully verified
the Proverb, Parturiunt montes.

appropriated to me the following lines, out of Young's divine poem, the Night Thoughts.

Come my ambitious, let us mount together,
To mount the Rambler, never can refufe.

After a fhort delay, fome incidental oc-currences afforded me a conjectural glimpfe that Hymeneus was afcending in the abrupt-nefs of extacy *. Sympathy affected me with fimilarity of fenfations and unifonal vibrations of mind. My own afcenfionary powers, which erft were relaxed with numbnefs, congealed with frigorifick torpor, and debilitated with the confequential langour of an ardent contention and zealous competition for fkit-tleary fame, received a temporary influx of fympathetical, momentary invigoration. The drowfinefs of hefitation † being thus wakened into refolve, I difpatched an ex-pert and fkillful plenipotentiary in queft of one of thofe nymphs who enjoy a perpetual fufceptibility of occafional pleafure. Hy-pertatus undertook the cure of my intellec-tual malady. He laid before me the tortu-ofities

* Ramb. No. 117.          † Idler.

ofities of imaginary rectitude, the complications of fimplicity, and afperities of
fmoothnefs ; he reprefented, that the fofteft
bloom of rofeate virginity repells the eye
with excrefcencies and difcolorations ; he
attempted to awaken the powers of diflike,
raife an artificial faftidioufnefs at the coarfe-
nefs of vulgar felicity, and to fill my imagination with phantoms of turpitude, naked
fkeletons of delight, pains of pleafure, and
deformities of beauty*. But he had not the
addrefs to adminifter, nor did he know
with what vehicles to difguife the catharticks
of the foul. At laft, the ambaffador of love
returned, introducing Perdita. Hypertatus continued ftill to harrafs me with monitory injunctions, and deter me with prohibitory fanctions; but gazing the meretricial
prefence, whofe charms would roufe the old
to fenfibility, and fubdue the rigourous to
foftnefs, I began to entertain a conjectural glimpfe, that Hypertatus was practifing
arts of fupplantation and detraction, and
that he was inftigated by the corrofions of
envy to poifon the banquet which he could
not tafte, and to blaft the harveft which he

F 2  had

* For this fentence, fee Ramb. No. 112.

had no right to reap. Therefore, that he might not intercept the regular maturation of my fchemes, I fhook off the drowfy equi-librations of undetermined counfels *, and carried Perdita to a private apartment.

And now ye, who liften with credulity to the whifpers of fancy, and purfue with eager-nefs the phantoms of hope, who expect that age will perform the promifes of youth, and that the deficiencies of the prefent day will be fupplied by the morrow; attend to the hiftory of the AUTHOR of Raffelas, prince of Abyffinia †.

As foon as the neceffary preliminary articles for an amicable congrefs were finally adjufted to the mutual fatisfaction of the contracting parties, Perdita eagerly co-operated to ripen barren volition into efficacy and power ‡. But alas! fuch helplefs deftitution, fuch difmal-inanity, fuch gloomy privation, fuch im-potent defire! the faculties of anticipation flumbered in defpondency, but the powers of pleafure mutinied not for employment §; and vain were all her fafcinating charms, and equally vain all my artificial ftimulations to

effectuate

---

* Ramb. No. 111.　　† Raffelas, Vol. 1. p. 1.
‡ Ramb. No. 116.　　§ Ramb. No. 133.

effectuate a proper and adequate reciprocation of civilities.    For the orbicular repofi-
tories of my powers, and teftimonials of my
majeftick forms - - - - -.

CRITICK.

Have done, Mr. J - - - - - n, for God's
fake have done.   We have had enough of
afcending ard reciting.   Befides, I guefs
what follows is neither fit for you to read
nor me to hear.   This, however, is not all
I find fault with.   Where the D---l! have
you collected all this trafh of hard words,
from what magazine or repofitory have you
raked together thefe perverfe terms and
abfurd phrafes, wherewith you have befpat-
tered me, who never did you any wrong,
at fo unmerciful a rate?   Some, I fee, are
of your own invention ;  for others you muft
have ranfacked the old mufty volumes of
former times, juftly difregarded when firft
written, and now defervedly forgotten.   The
reft I perceive you have gleaned up, with
infinite pains, from Greek and Latin, from
fcholaftick writers, and books on the abftrufe
fciences.   And you think you have done a
mighty pretty feat, that you have perform-

ed an eminent service to learning, when you have wriggled, in over head and shoulders, a new-fashioned long-tailed word, what in your own phrase I would call a *vermicular* word, or a dark term of art, without considering whether it be proper to the subject, suited to the capacity of your readers, or indeed whether it be an English word or not. You are the unfittest person of any I know for what you have undertaken, to compile a dictionary. Though 'tis indeed no wonder you should be employed by bookfellers in such a work.

Besides, you are wholly ignorant of what is the main part, and makes the chiefest excellence of stile, I mean the choice of words. For no where have you erred so grossly as in your Ramblers, notwithstanding you had such admirable models before you, in the writings of Steele and Addison, whom you have been so impudent as to call your great predeceffors. What would they say, were they to rise from the dead! what opinion do you think they would entertain of the present age, that can tamely bear such a comparison!

I have

I have heard your fkill in lexicography to be highly extolled: But cannot imagine what you would underftand by it. I am affured you know nothing of the true fpirit of the Englifh tongue, which delights in words of one, of two, or at moft of three fyllables derived from the old Saxon ftock; and doth not willingly admit any Latin words whatever, at leaft in the common ftile, unlefs they come to us through the channel of the French, and have been long, if I may fo exprefs myfelf, denizons among us. But you, without any difcernment or diftinction, have huddled in all the Latin words you could fcrape together, to which you could by any means affix an Englifh termination.

You really feem to me poffeffed with a fort of madnefs. 'Tis in my opinion a melancholy. And that windy vapour, or rather watery humour which puffs you up, and makes you look fo round and fair, is, in truth, the worft fymptom of your diftemper. 'Tis not impoffible you may have many admirers in the prefent times, who are either ignorant of your calamity, or equally fmitten with the fame difeafe. For

F 4                    ought

ought I know, fome may give you the name of the excellent Rambler, and may join you in calling the productions of thofe incomparable wits, Sheffield and Lanfdown, pages of inanity, one of your d---m--d execrable Latin terms, and another of thofe numberlefs evils with which you have fo peftered me for this hour paft. But truft me, thefe muft be pedants like yourfelf. Befides, their applaufes cannot be difinterefted. They either look for a return, or praife their own refemblance in you. All men of good tafte and judgment, take my word on't, laugh at you, pity you, and hold your writings on the fcore of their folemn and affected foppery in high contempt.

Truely, Mr. J-----n, you appear to me, a very unhappy perfon, who have not one real friend in fo large a city, and among fo numerous an acquaintance. Not one, who, in the courfe of fo many years, has had the honefty to inform you of the dangerous way you were in, or the generofity to clear you of that monftrous gathering of impure trafh which will certainly burft you afunder one time or other. On the contrary, it feems, from your vanity and felf-fufficience, they

have

have flattered you, and told you, you were in a good confirmed ſtate of health, though you were all the while in the moſt deplorable ſituation.

For my own part I thought at firſt to have laugh'd at you; but that torrent of hard words you poured out upon me all at unawares, quite ſtunned and overwhelmed me at laſt. They made me very drunk and ſick, I grew giddy, and ſhould actually have vomited, had I not interrupted you. Truth is, I ſhall not reckon on being my own man again, till I have thrown up every ſyllable I have heard from you. Would to God I could ſee Dr. Monro: he has been buſied all his life-time, in looking after crazy, crack-brain'd fellows like yourſelf. He may poſſibly do you ſervice, provided your caſe lie not beyond the reach of medicine.

Well, I ſee a gentleman coming towards us, whom I take, by his dreſs, to be a phyſician. It is not Monro. But whoever he be, 'twill do no harm to conſult him.

Sir, preſuming you, from your appearance, a phyſician, though I have not the honour of being known to you, I make bold to conſult you on the caſe of my friend

Mr.

Mr. J-----n here, who is extremely ill with the difeafe of ftrange words. Not to mince the matter, but let it reft between you and I, he is taken with a fort of madnefs. Be fo good as order fomething for him, and I'll warrant you, if ever he recover his fenfes, you fhall be liberally rewarded for your trouble.

### First Physician.

When fhall the laurel and the vocal ftring
Refume their honours? When fhall we behold
The tuneful tongue, the Promethéan hand
Afpire to ancient praife? Alas! how faint,
How flow the dawn of beauty and of truth
Breaks the reluctant fhades of Gothic night
Which yet involve the nations! Long they groan'd
Beneath the furies of rapacious force *;

* The reader cannot but obferve the different manner in which I have treated the two Lexiphane-fes. Mr. Johnfon's matter and fenfe is fometimes fo excellent, and his reflections now and then fo juft, and at the fame time fo uncommon, that it hides, in fome meafure, the abfurdity of the ftile, which becomes, on that account, the more danger-ous. I was therefore obliged to *parody* him, and in order to fhew his hard words and affectation in a more glaring and ridiculous point of view, apply them to the

Oft at the gloomy north, with iron-fwarms
Tempeftuous pouring from her frozen caves,
Blafted th' Italian fhore, and fwept the works
Of liberty and wifdom down the gulph

the meaneft, the moft ludicrons and phantaftical objects I could well think on. But fuch a conduct was by
no means neceffary with A——de our poetical Lexiphanes. His words and efpecially his phrafes are
generally fo execrable, and his meaning, where any
can be pick'd out, always fo triffling; in fhort, he
has *imbibed* fo much of Plato's nonfenfe, but fo little
of his *gracious manner*, as I think he fomewhere calls
it, that I concluded bare and thofe even faithful
quotations from him, were the very beft expofure of
the ridiculoufnefs and futility of his compofition.

The above is, in my opinion, one of the leaft ex-
ceptionable paffages in his whole rhapfody. This
is doublefs giving him fair play, and we fhall now
examine it by the rules, I will not fay of criticifm,
but of common fenfe. In the firft and third lines,
we have no lefs than four enigmas or riddles, every
jot as hard as that of the Sphynx, though I don't
fay they require an Oedipus to expound them. Before a common reader can underftand them, he muft
either be told, or recollect the ftory of Apollo and
Daphné, that Apollo was the God of poetry, that
the laurel was one of his favourite *infignia*, and that
poets ufed to be crowned with it at publick folemni-
ties, or when they rehearfed their works. By the
*vocal ftring*, one may eafily underftand mufick, in-
ftrumental only, and even in that cafe a *metonimy*,
a part for the whole. I confefs myfelf fomewhat at

a lofs

Of all-devouring night. As long immur'd
In noon-tide darkness by the glimmering lamp,
Each muse and each fair science pin'd away
The sordid hours : while foul, barbarian hands

a loss about the *tuneful tongue*. It's best and most obvious meaning is poetry ; but we had the *laurel* before ; and our *British Lucretius* can never be guilty of such gross and needless *tautology*. Therefore if he has any meaning at all, a thing however not very frequent with our author, he must mean vocal musick or singing. I shall not pretend to determine, whether *ancient* or *modern singing* have aspired to the greatest degree of praise ; but this I know, that the modern's have been at infinitely more pains to procure good singers. For I never heard that the ancients went to that excess of luxury and refinement in musick, as to deprive the male singers of their *virile powers*. It had been no loss to poetry, whatever it might have been to physick, if the Doctor's father had aspired to modern praise as a singer.

But the most puzzling task is the *Promethéan band*; if, however, we happen to recollect the old fable of Prometheus, who molded a man of clay, and stole fire out of heaven to animate him ; we may, perhaps, give a shrewd guess, that *statuary* is meant by it.

Such an ordinary poet as Virgil, having occasion to mention statuary, contents himself, with doing it in this dull and simple manner,

Excudent alii spirantia mollius aera ;
Credo equidem, vivos ducent de marmore vultus.

Which

Their myfteries profan'd, unftrung the lyre,
And chain'd the foaring pinion down to earth.
At laft the Mufes rofe, and fpurn'd their bonds,
And wildly warbling, fcatter'd, as they flew,

Which Dryden, a trauflator, only fit for fuch an author, renders in a ftrain equally infipid.

> Let others better mould the running mafs
> Of metals, and inform the breathing brafs ;
> And foften into flefh a marble face.

Yet it may be obferved, that the fable of Prometheus, being an article in the publick religion, Virgil might have ufed this *enigma* with a much better
chance of being underftood.

Having thus expounded the riddles, let us fee
what is next to be done. The queftion is afked,
when fhall *finging* and *ftatuary afpire to ancient praife,*
by which he either underftands the praifes of antiquity, or the praife thofe arts obtained in the times
of antiquity ? The firft is downright nonfenfe, the
laft is obfcurely quaintly and affectedly expreffed.
It is alfo afked, when fhall *poetry* and *fiddling refume
their honours ?* Pray, did the Doctor ever read that
a poet and a fidler (though in Homer's time the two
profeffions were joined in one) were ever feated on a
bench like a brace of trading juftices, and ftiled
their honours and worfhips ? Or would he have them
honoured fo in our days, and have he and fignor
Giardini, any ambition to fucceed their worfhips
Welfh and Fielding ? But, perhaps, he means only
to enquire when they fhall be honoured and refpect-
ed

Their blooming wreaths from fair Valclufa's
    bow'rs
To Arno's myrtle border and the fhore
Of foft Parthenope. But ftill the rage
Of dire ambition and gigantic pow'r,
From public aims and from the bufy walk
Of civil commerce, drove the bolder train
Of penetrating fcience to the cells,

                    Where

ed as formerly, but expreffed in his ufual quaint
Lexiphanick manner.

    The ftuff which follows about *beauty* and *truth*;
that in this line are *dawning*, and in the next *groan-*
*ing*, though here another ambiguity arifes, for 'tis
difficult to fay, whether 'tis the *nations* that *groan*,
or the two pretty little miffes, *beauty* and *truth*,
that lie crying and blubbering under the *furies*
of *force*, but I think the latter interpretation
more agreeable to our author's manner; I fay
the ftuff that follows is fo abftracted and remote
from the common thoughts and expreffions of men,
that 'tis only proper for his abfurd rhapfody, and
could have place no-where but in his own phantaf-
tick imagination. But 'tis really wafting time and
paper to criticize fuch an author. Befides, a fenfible reader wants no criticifm upon him, and thofe
who admire or can even with patience read him, will
not be the better for it. Reafoning from any principles
would be as much thrown away upon them as upon
Whitefield's followers, who are equally edified and
affected by the words Samaria or Mefopotamia, pronounced with a certain twang, and by the moft pa-
thetick difcourfes on repentance or a future ftate.

Where ſtudious eaſe conſumes the ſilent hour
In ſhadowy ſearches and unfruitful care.
Thus from their guardians torn, the tender arts
Of mimic fancy and harmonious joy,
To prieſtly domination and the luſt
Of lawleſs courts, their amiable toil
For three inglorious ages have reſign'd,
In vain reluctant : and Torquato's tongue
Was tun'd for ſlaviſh pæans at the throne
Of tinſel pomp : and Raphael's magic hand
Effus'd its fair creation to enchant
The fond adoring herd in Latian fanes
To bind belief ; while on their proſtrate necks
The ſable tyrant plants his heel ſecure.
But now behold ! the radiant æra dawns,
When freedom's ample fabric, fix'd at length
For endleſs years on Albion's happy ſhore
In full proportion, once more ſhall extend
To all the kindred pow'rs of ſocial bliſs
A common manſion, a parental roof.
There ſhall the Virtues, there ſhall Wiſdom's
     train
Their long-loſt friends rejoining, as of old,
Imbrace the ſmiling family of arts,
The Muſes and the Graces.   Then no more
Shall vice, diſtracting their delicious gifts
To aims abhorr'd, with high diſtaſte and ſcorn
Turn from their charms the philoſophic eye,
The patriot-boſom ; then no more the paths
Of public care or intellectual toil,
                    Alone

Alone by footſteps haughty and ſevere
In gloomy ſtate be trod : th' harmonious Muſe
And her perſuaſive ſiſters then ſhall plant
Their ſhelt'ring laurels o'er the bleak aſcent,
And ſcatter flow'rs along the rugged way.
Arm'd with the lyre, already have we dar'd
To pierce divine philoſophy's retreats,
And teach the Muſe her lore ; already ſtrove
Their long-divided honours to unite,
While temp'ring this deep argument we ſang
Of truth and beauty.   Now the ſame taſk
Impends ; now urging our ambitious toil,
We haſten to recount the various ſprings
Of adventitious pleaſure, which adjoin
Their grateful influence to the prime effect
Of objects grand or beauteous, and inlarge
The complicated joy.   The ſweets of ſenſe,
Do they not oft with ſweet acceſſion flow,
To raiſe harmonious fancy's native charm ?
So while we taſte the fragrance of the roſe,
Glows not her bluſh the fairer ? While we view
Amid the noontide walk a limped rill
Guſh thro' the trickling herbage, to the thirſt·
Of ſummer yielding the delicious draught
Of cool refreſhment ; o'er the moſſy brink
Shines not the ſurface clearer, and the waves
With ſweeter muſic murmur as they flow ?

CRITICK,

CRITICK.

I've made a confounded miftake here. 'Twas well I did not give him a fee, as I was once thinking to do. This Phyfician is madder than the patient, and has more need of a prefcription. What he fpouts forth fhould be poetry by the found. I mean blank verfe. But I don't underftand one word on't. Doctor, I fee you are juft now got into the clouds, where, by cuftom, time out of mind, people are freed from the flavery of talking fenfe. I beg you'd defcend from your prefent altitudes, and endeavour to earn the fee I promifed you.

FIRST PHYSICIAN.

Say, why was man fo eminently rais'd
Amid the vaft creation ; why ordain'd
Thro' life and death to dart his piercing eye,
With thoughts beyond the limit of his frame ;
But that th' Omnipotent might fend him forth
In fight of mortal and immortal pow'rs,
As on a boundlefs theatre, to run
The great career of juftice ; to exalt
His gen'rous aim to all diviner deeds ;
To chafe each partial purpofe from his breaft ;
And thro' the mifts of paffion and of fenfe,

G                                          And

And thro' the toffing tide of chance and pain,.
To hold his courfe unfalt'ring, while his voice
Of truth and virtue,. up the fteep afcent
Of nature, calls him to his high reward,
Th' applauding fmile of heav'n? Elfe wherefore
      burns
In mortal bofoms this unquenched hope,
That breaths from day to day fublimer things,
And mocks poffeffion? wherefore darts the mind,.
With fuch refiftlefs ardour to embrace
Majeftic forms; impatient to be free,
Spurning the grofs controul of wilful might;
Proud of the ftrong contention of her toils;
Proud to be daring? Who but rather turns
To heav'n's broad fire his unconftrained view,
Than to the glimmering of a waxen flame?
Who that, from Alpine heights, his lab'ring eye
Shoots round the wide horizon, to furvey
Nilus or Ganges rowling his bright wave
Thro' mountains, plains, thro' empires black
      with fhade,
And continents of fand; will turn his gaze
To mark the windings of a fcanty rill
That murmurs at his feet? The high-born foul
Difdains to reft her heav'n-afpiring wing
Beneath its native quarry. Tir'd of earth
And this diurnal fcene, fhe fprings aloft
Thro' fields of air; purfues the flying ftorm;
Rides on the volley'd lightning thro' the heav'ns;
Or yok'd with whirlwinds and the northern blaft,
                  Sweeps.

Sweeps the long tract of day. Then high fhe
 foars
The blue profound, and hovering round the fun
Beholds him pouring the redundant ftream
Of light; beholds his unrelenting fway
Bend the reluctant planets to abfolve
The fated rounds of time. Thence far effus'd
She darts her fwiftnefs up the long career
Of devious comets; thro' its burning figns
Exulting meafures the perennial wheel
Of nature, and looks back on all the ftars,
Whofe blended light, as with a milky zone,
Invefts the orient. Now amaz'd fhe views
Th' empyreal wafte, where happy fpirits hold,
·Beyond this concave heav'n, their calm abode ;
And fields of radiance, whofe unfading light
Has travell'd the profound fix thoufand years,
Nor yet arrives in fight of mortal things.
Ev'n on the barriers of the world untir'd
She meditates th' eternal depth below ;
Till, half recoiling, down the headlong fteep
She plunges; foon o'erwhelm'd and fwallow'd up
In that immenfe of being. There her hopes
Reft at the fatal goal. For from the birth
Of mortal man, the fovereign Maker faid,
That not in humble nor in brief delight
Not in the fading echoes of renown,
Pow'r's purple robes, nor pleafure's flow'ry lap,
The foul fhould find enjoyment: but from thefe
Turning difdainful to an equal good,

Thro' all th' afcent of things inlarge her view,
Till every bound at length fhould difappear,
And infinite perfection clofe the fcene.

## CRITICK.

I afk pardon, Doctor, for having interrupted you. I fee you are very bufy at
prefent. I fhall take an opportunity, when
you are more at leifure, to wait on you with
the patient.

## FIRST PHYSICIAN.

Wait awhile,
My curious friends! and let us firft arrange
In proper orders your promifcuous throng.
    Behold the foremoft band; of flender thought,
And eafy faith; whom flatt'ring fancy fooths
With lying fpectres, in themfelves to view
Illuftrious forms of excellence and good,
That fcorn the manfion. With exulting hearts
They fpread their fpurious treafures to the fun,
And bid the world admire! but chief the glance
Of wifhful envy draws their joy-bright eyes,
And lifts with felf-applaufe each lordly brow.
In number boundlefs as the blooms of fpring,
Behold their glaring idols, empty fhades
By fancy gilded o'er, and then fet up
For adoration. Some in learning's garb,
With formal-band, and fable-cinctur'd gown,
                                            And

And rags of mouldy volumes.   Some elate
With martial fplendor, fteely pikes and fwords
Of coftly frame,  and gay Pœnician robes
Inwrought with flow'ry gold, affume the port
Of ftately valour : lift'ning by his fide
There ftands a female form ; to her, with looks
Of earneft import, pregnant with amaze,
He talks of deadly deeds, of breaches, ftorms,
And fulph'rous  mines,  and  ambufh :  then at
    once
Breaks off, and fmiles to fee her look fo pale,
And afks fome wond'ring queftion of her fears.
Others of graver mien ;  behold, adorn'd
With holy enfigns,  how fublime they move
And bending oft their fanctimonious eyes,
Take homage of the fimple-minded throng;
Ambaffadors of heav'n !

### CRITICK.

This is paft all fufferance.   Patient Griz-
zel herfelf could not endure fuch a huf-
band.   How fhall I manage to get rid of
this poetical fop.   I had beft quarrel with
him on pretence he affronts me by brand-
ifhing his fift, and making mouths in the
fury and extacy of his rehcaffal.

### FIRST PHYSICIAN.

What, when to raife the meditated fcene,
The flame of paffion, thro' the ftruggling foul
Deep-kindled, fhows acrofs that fudden blaze
The object of it's rapture, vaft of fize,
With fiercer colours and a night of fhade?
What?*

### CRITICK.                          ,

What Sir, do you fhake your fift at me,
laugh at me, and threaten me, all in one
breath?

* The reft of this paffage is as follows :

Like a ftorm from their capacious bed
The founding feas o'erwhelming, when the might
Of thefe eruptions, working from the depth
Of man's ftrong apprehenfion, fhakes his frame
Ev'n to the bafe; from ev'ry naked fenfe
Of pain or pleafure, diffipating all
Opinion's feeble cov'rings, and the veil
Spun from the cobweb fafhion of the times
To hide the feeling heart? Then nature fpeaks
Her genuine language, and the words of men
Big with the very motion of our fouls,
Declare with what accumulated force
Th' impetuous nerve of paffion urges on
The native weight and energy of things.

I have often admired this fublime piece of nonfenfe, and endeavoured to find out its meaning; but
it hath hitherto baffled the outmoft exertion of my
*intellectual powers.* Whoever fhall give a confiftent
explication of it, and in a few words, for I bar a
commentary; *Erit mihi Magnus Apollo.*

breath? Know Sir, I am not a man to put
up with fuch ufage? Befides, Sir, I have
very particular bufinefs with this gentleman,
and if you don't take yourfelf away, fhall
make bold to apply that you wont like,
to what my friend here calls a very refpectable part of your body *.

* This language, perhaps, requires fome apology, when applied to one, who though a very affected poet, may be, and I doubt not is a very worthy
gentleman. As for the poet himfelf, I can only
hope he will look down upon it, with that noble
and fovereign difdain fo well becoming our modern
Milton and Britifh Lucretius, for fo he is called.
To the publick I make the following excufe. Let
the fituation of the Critick be confidered, one who
had never heard of the Poem or Poet, and, taking
him for a madman, earneftly defirous to break off
the rehearfal, and it will be owned no other expedi-
ent could fo naturally be thought on. Grant it were
a *dignus vindice nodus*, yet there was no *Vindex*, no
*God*, who could be introduced with any propriety.
Had the Critick, indeed, been acquainted with the
allegory which

  *Old Harmodius wont to teach*
  *His early age,*

he might have pretended to *appall him*, by *gazing*
the *godlike prefence* of the *genius of humankind*, to *lure*
him away with the charms of the *heavenly partner*, the
*fovereign fair*, or the *gay companion* the *fair Euphrofyne*,

### First Physician.

Thou my prime part profane with defperate
    toe,
By heavens, bafe caitiff, thou fhalt be amerc'd,
And when in durance vile defpair fhall grafp
Thy agonizing bofom, thou fhalt learn,
Then thou fhalt learn.-----

### Critick.

Learn! What fhould I learn from thee,
poetical fop! But confider Sir, (I wont
quarrel with this madman if I can help it)
here's company coming, and fure were you
in your fenfes you would not be feen in fuch
extafy for the world. I befeech you go re-
hearfe elfewhere.

A happy riddance faith.    *Exit* 1ft *Phyf.*
                         But

or he might e'en have frightened him off with a *vi-
fion* of the fon of *Nemefis* the *Tormentor,* the *fiend
abhorr'd,* and *horrid vifage* all *Dramatis perfonæ,* in
that allegory, that quinteffence of bombaft and un-
fathomable nonfenfe.

I haye, indeed, heard fome of his warmeft
admirers own, that allegory to be fomewhat dark
and obfcure, yet they ftill continued to believe in
his perfpicuity and fublimity. See the Athenian
Creed in Witherfpoon's Effays.

But who comes here now. Another Phyfician as I live; with the fame garb, equipage, and accoutrements as the laft. Pray heaven he be not a poet too. It looks very like my good friend and acquaintance, Doctor -------. It is he, and next to Monro, the very man I wifhed to meet with.

Dear Doctor, the pleafanteft adventure in the world I have to tell you. Here's my friend, J-------n, our Englifh Lexiphanes; he is very ill indeed, he is terribly afflicted with the difeafe of hard long-tailed words, drawn from the Greek and Latin languages, or terms of art only proper in abftrufe fciences, but ufed by him in common converfation, and in weekly papers, written, like the Spectators, for the amufement of ladies; in fhort, he has made fuch a hotch-potch of our mother-tongue, you would hardly know it again. He fpeaks as never man fpake before him.

#### SECOND PHYSICIAN.

Pooh! is that all! court, country and city, the high judicatures of the nation, and the Robin-hood fociety are all alike infected
with

with this diftemper; you meet with fuch words in fpeeches from the ---------- and addreffes from both --------, you hear them from the grave folemn politician, who harangues by the hour in a certain affembly, and from the weekly difputant, who is filenced at the end of five minutes, by the knock of a hammer. This difeafe is as catching as the fmall-pox, no-body efcapes it, fome even chufe to be inoculated for it; as obftinate as the great ones, it ftays with you, and like the Portugueze or Spaniards, who reckon their fashionable evil a mark of gentility, no-body takes any pains to get rid of it. But in what part of the world have you been pray, that you did not know all this before ?

### CRITICK.

Abroad faith, and I'm glad on't, 'thas let me efcape one infection at leaft.

### SECOND PHYSICIAN.

But is this your pleafant adventure ?

CRI-

CRITICK.

No! no: the rant's a coming as Bays
fays, 'tis only the *proemial* part of my ftory,
as Lexiphanes has it. You muft know, being once fo fituated, that I had no accefs to
any Englifh books excepting the Rambler,
if indeed you call that an Englifh one, and ·
having no better way to employ myfelf in,
I made a hard fhift to read through and underftand it with the help of a dictionary, for
the words, though ending like Englifh ones,
founded plaguily like Greek or Latin, and
were in truth nothing elfe at bottom. However, it gave me a good opinion of the man's
underftanding; I faw he had fenfe and meaning, though ftrangely wrapt up in a mift of
hard words ; there was deep obfervation,
fhrewd remarks on life and manners, and a
good infight into the characters of men.
Soon after, on coming to London, I found
means to be introduced to his acquaintance,
curious to obferve more nearly fo queer a
being, and found him a greater oddity than
I could have imagined. He has juft now
been reading to me, part of a work, which
he calls a *novel exhibition, purely virginal,*
and

and never *critically furveyed*; but fuch an
*exhibition!* Jacob Behmen, Flood, Alex-
ander Rofs, all the Rofycrucian Philofophers,
in fhort, cannot match it. After I had ftopt
his recital, my patience quite wore out by
fuch odious ftuff, a prig of a Doctor came
by, equipped for all the world, I afk your
pardon, Sir, juft like yourfelf; a large wig,
his hat under his arm, a black coat, a fword
by his fide, and a coach following him without a footman behind it. Defirous to cure
fo valuable a perfon of a fort of phrenzy or
madnefs *, that rendered all his other excel-

* The fatyr in this place cannot be thought ex-
travagant, or too fevere, by thofe who duly confider
that principle in the human mind, whence all faulty
and remarkable fingularities, whether in drefs, be-
haviour, or language, moft commonly proceed; a
man's fond and overweaning conceit of himfelf; and
ridiculous overbearing contempt of people about
him; which is faid to be the cafe with our Lexiphanes. This every fober perfon muft allow to be
a fort of madnefs in difguife; but perhaps too common, as well as too harmlefs to require a confine-
ment in Bedlam. Moreover I am juftified in it by
the authority of Lucian, who in all the correfpond-
ing paffages, afcribes the fame diftemper to his Lexiphanes, and cures him in the fame manner, by a
potion originally prepared for an infane patient.
Cer-

lent endowments good for nothing, I accof-
ted this Doctor, I defired him to prefcribe,
and promifed him a fee, but inftead of anfwering like a reafonable creature, or being

---

Cervantes too, with equal humour and judgment,
reprefents Lexiphanicifm, or an admiration of Lexiphanick writings, as the firft fymptom of Don Quix-
ote's madnefs, and through the whole courfe of it,
paints him a compleat Lexiphanes. In a word, the
greateft wits in all ages, and in all nations, have
concurred, and feem to have taken a peculiar pleafure in making that character the object of their moft
pointed ridicule. Lucian and Cervantes I have already mentioned ; Rabelais has a very pleafant paffage to the fame purpofe, where Pantagruel meets a
Limoufin fcholar near the gates of Paris, and after
hearing him *Lexiphanize* for fome time, cures him at
laft, and brings him back to his native gibberifh by
a fqueeze in the throat ; Butler too, from whom I
have taken the motto, defcribes Hudibras in that
character, and in a manner quite new and original.
Neither has it efcaped Plautus and Shakefpear, the
one in his *Miles Gloriofus*, and the other in Ancient
Piftol. I only wonder that Swift has never introduced this character in all his numerous writings.
How muft it have fhone when painted by his mafterly
pen. But he appears to have thought it an object
too facred for ridicule, though he has made very free
with others feemingly more fo ; for he has wrote a-
gainft the thing, *Lexiphanicifm* I mean, in a very
grave and ferious ftile. 'Tis perhaps for this reafon
that

awakened by a fubject which commonly makes all Doctors a little attentive, he went on repeating fome verfes, for, I fuppofe, he had been engaged in the rehearfal before, which I am fure were every way blank, for I could neither make head nor tail of 'em.

## SECOND PHYSICIAN.

Do you remember any of thofe verfes?

## CRITICK.

How the d---l can I, for I did not under-ftand one fentence, not one line. O yes; now I recollect, he invoked the genius of ancient Greece, talked of Greek and At-tick Lore, raved about Power's pur-ple robes, and Pleafure's hairy, pooh, I mean flowery lap, then made an hide-

ous

that Young, who in his old age, or dotage, dege-nerated into a downright Lexiphanes, having always had a twang that way, calls him, in the effay on *Original Compofition*, addreffed to another Lexiphanes the *Soul-harrowing Richardjon*, an *Infantine Genius*. The pompous Pedant too, who is my Hero, for the fame caufe, I imagine, fpeaks fo flightingly both of Swift and Butler in his Idlers, not bearing to fee the thing he is fo fond of expofed by the one, and his own likenefs drawn by the other.

ous ado, about a meditated ſcene and a flame of paſſion ſtruggling through the ſoul, which deep kindled, ſhews a ſudden blaze acroſs, vaſt of ſize, with fiercer colours, and a night of ſhade. Ay, theſe were ſome of his laſt words, for juſt then.----

### SECOND PHYSICIAN.

Ha! ha! ha! By all that's good this muſt be A------, for I remember ſomething very like it, in his poem on the Pleaſures of Imagination, which he calls a prime ſubject, importing moſt a poet's name.

### CRITICK.

Ay, ay, the very ſame. Prime is a great word with him. For being obliged to pretend a quarrel to get free from his nonſenſe, he dared me to profane his prime part, as he called it, and told me when deſpair graſped my agonizing boſom, I ſhould learn, then I ſhould learn ------. But this poem, this Pleaſures of Imagination, is it of any note, is it held in requeſt, hath it ſold, or doth it ſtill lie on the Bookſeller's ſtall?

SECOND

SECOND PHYSICIAN.

What queftions are thefe ? Where have you lived thefe laft twenty years ? Hath it fold, or is it in requeft ? Why it hath gone through numberlefs editions. 'Tis the prime poem, and he is the prime poet of our age and nation. He is admired, quoted, commented upon by our men of modern tafte.

CRITICK.

Good God ! fuch men of tafte ! what age is this we live in ! That men fhould ever admire any thing, efpecially poetry, which they cannot underftand ! Yet, perhaps, for that very reafon they do it. 'Tis become a ftrange world, this of ours. Pray heaven I foon get abroad again*.

* I had faid in a former note, *reafoning would be thrown away on the admirers of this poet.* That this cenfure may not be thought too fevere, I fhall here add an obfervation, obvious to the meaneft capacity, and applicable to all fubjects. It is this. As plainnefs or perfpicuity is the firft beauty and greateft perfection in writing, fo its contrary, darknefs and obfcurity is its greateft fault and deformity. And I fhall fupport it, by the greateft authority, one of them, the Englifh tongue can afford. I mean the
famous

SECOND PHYSICIAN.

Nay, he is ftiled our Britifh Lucretius, and even pronounced by our prefent criticks, not inferior to Milton, Dryden, Pope, in a word, all our beft poets fince the reftoration.

H                   CRI-

_famous Burnet of the Charterhoufe, who in his preface to the third book of his Theory, has the following paffage. " As to the ftyle, I always endeavour to exprefs myfelf in a plain and perfpicuous manner; that the reader may not lofe time, nor wait too long to know my meaning. I would not willingly," continues he, " give any one the trouble of reading a period twice over, to know the fenfe of it ; left, when he comes to know it, he fhould not think it a recompence for his pains." If fo great a man, writing on the grandeft and fublimeft of all themes, the original formation of this our World out of a fhapelefs Chaos, its firft deftruction by a general deluge, its laft by an univerfal confiagration, and its renovation into a new and more glorious Heaven and Earth, and the final confummation of All Things; if fuch a man I fay, in fuch a fubject, require plainnefs and perfpicuity, as fo neceffary and indifpenfable, what muft we think of an ordinary author, who, writing on a common fubject, and in poetry too, labours in a manner to be dark, affected and obfcure._

CRITICK.

Our Britifh Lucretius! The Roman, if he can be found fault with for any thing, 'tis for being too fimple and unadorned *,

* This is pretty nearly Mr. Hume's opinion of Lucretius, in his Effay on *Simplicity* and *Refinement.* He fays, in the fame place, that an excefs in the latter is more dangerous and more to be guarded a- gainft than an excefs in the former; and adds, that even then, above twenty years ago, there were fymp- toms of an approaching decline of tafte, both in France and England. How truely he hath prophe- cied, at leaft, with refpect to the latter, let the Ramblers, Pleafures of Imagination, &c. juftify.

Now I have mentioned this gentleman, for whofe character and talents I entertain the higheft venera- tion, I cannot pafs this opportunity of making him an acknowledgment for fuffering his illuftrious name to appear in the margin, for the moft part, in fuch bad company. But 'tis only for a few words I thought affected, and it was his great and fo juftly deferved reputation that made me take notice of them at all. A like apology may be thought due to Dr. Robertfon, for mentioning *Mas David Black's Declinature*, which being perhaps the only unjuftifi- able word in his hiftory, and a Scotch law term be- fide, 'tis probable he got from his friend, *Mas John Davidfon*, the Clerk. See Appendix to the Hiftory of Scotland, Vol. II. But there are others who have gone thro',

whereas the other, if he has any fenfe or
meaning at all, which, by the way, is very
much to be queftioned, it is wholly hid under a fuperfluity of ridiculous fantaſtick ornaments, that 'tis with great difficulty come
at, and when you do, 'tis good for nothing,
and you regret your trouble. He refem-
bles a little dirty ill-looking Baboon, buried
under a huge ill-made birth-day fuit, and
when you have ftript him bare of his tawdry
covering, you meet with nothing but what
difgufts the eye and offends the nofe, and
every other fenfe about you. In fhort, 'tis
hardly poffible to name two writers, whofe
tafte and manner jar fo much, and are fo
directly contrary to one another. But who
is the great genius, pray, that hit upon fo
happy a comparifon?

H 2 Second

thro', as Lexiphanes-fomewhere fays, *full as fatiguing a
ſervice of celebrity*, as either of thofe gentlemen, and
who fhould have appeared oftener in the margin
than both, had not the notes and extracts, taken
from their writings, been loft, (fee the Preface)
though I fhould hardly have troubled them with
an apology for the freedom.

## SECOND PHYSICIAN.

A perfonage of great note, I affure you, one of *fignal celebrity* for *critical powers*. He writes on poetry and painting *. You're a great admirer of rhyme, I know, and cannot relifh the blank verfe at leaft of our days. But were you to read him, you would foon alter your opinion; he would foon convince you, rhyme is fit for nothing but madrigals, epigrams and acrofticks.

## CRITICK.

So he's a warm ftickler for blank verfe. I thought fo. But I fincerely believe this blank verfe has been the great corrupter of our tafte and language, both in profe and poetry. For my part, I have for fome time made it a fort of rule with me, to read nothing of that kind except Milton, whofe words, ftyle and meafure, are fo much his own, and fo well fuited to the loftinefs of his fubject, that they fet him equally above all criticifm and imitation. 'Tis true, I have read Dr. A------- elegant poem on health, as well as a very happy imitation of it, by

Mr.

* Daniel Webb, Efq.

Mr. D-------- on agriculture. They are
both fimple and natural, and have few or no
hard words in them, but for that very reafon, perhaps, are lefs fought for than others
written in the fame manner. Yet with all
the merit the poem on health undoubtedly
poffeffes, I fhould think it wrong to liken
it to thofe noble productions, Buckingham's
Effay on Poetry, Rofcommon's on tranflated
Verfe, and Pope's on Criticifm, all didactick poems. Though 'twere granted in e-
very thing elfe equal, this very circumftance
of it's being written in blank verfe, would
give it the difadvantage. That manner
does very well in tragedy, whofe ftyle approaches nearly to profe; for which reafon
it muft be unfit for every other fort of poetry. Befides, properly fpeaking, it is no
verfe at all. Verfe comes from the Latin
word *vertere*, to turn. Now if there be nothing in the meafure which informs the ear
when the verfes *turn* and *return*, or when
one verfe ends and other begins, it furely
does not deferve that title. This is evident-
ly the cafe with moft of our modern blank
pieces: did not the compofitor carefully
place one line of ten fyllables under another

of the fame length, but print them in the ufual manner, we fhould never find them out to be poetry, but fhould be foon con-vinced they were bad profe. Whereas, print the ancient Hexameter and modern rhyme as you pleafe, the Dactyle and Spon-dee on the one hand, and the return of found on the other, can never fuffer the moft in-different ear to miftake.

But I fhall not infift much on this topick, feeing it is only a difpute about words. But our admirers of blank verfe, complain that rhyme is a bondage, and lays too great a reftraint on the poet. This is only faying, in other words, he is no poet at all, or is too lazy to be a good one. The meafure of the ancients feems to have been a greater bondage than our rhyme ; it was certainly fo to Virgil, who has not left one imperfect verfe in his Paftorals or Georgicks, though many in his Æneid, which did not receive his laft hand, as we learn from this circum-ftance, though hardly from any other. However, we do not hear that complaint from any of them. But the truth is, in this very reftraint and bondage lies the fuperior excellence of rhyme. It is great merit, and

it

it gives mighty fatisfaction, to overcome a preffing difficulty, and to overcome it in fuch a manner that no traces of it are to be feen.  All the beauty and grace of writing depends on this principle.  To choofe fuch words, and place them in fuch an order, that every common reader fhall think he can do the fame, till he come to try it, and then finds himfelf greatly unequal to the tafk: fuch a man muft needs entertain a higher opinion of the writer who does this, than of him in whom he perceives pains and labour at every ftep he takes. On the other hand, a perfon acquainted with the hardfhips of compofition, muft receive infinite pleafure from a piece that feems to have been finifhed at one happy touch, without correction or labour, but which he knows from experience, muft have coft the author extreme pains to bring to that pitch of perfection.  Dryden, Pope, and many others have written in rhyme, with all the eafe and fluency of profe, not to fay, blank verfe; and I need not afk you, that know thefe things fo well, who have taken the greateft pains, and who have overcome the greateft difficulties. But fhould it be granted that rhyme is too heavy a bur-

then,

blank verfe, on the other hand, is as much too light an one; our language naturally falls into Iambicks, and any man who can reckon his ten fingers, may put a news-paper into blank verfe in as many minutes. But were there no other, this reafon alone would induce me to give the preference to rhyme. For rhyme, even in our degenerate days, when all true tafte feems to be banifhed, and nothing but grimace and affectation prevail in its room, leads to a fimpler and eafier expreffion, and does not require to diftinguifh it from profe, any of Lexiphanes's hard words, or Thompfon's ill-jointed, worfe-founding compounds.

## J - - - - - N.

Your fentiments and mine are, in this article, totally confonant and entirely confentaneous. For in order to maintain the dignification of blank verfe, and fupport its requifite exaltation over profe, our poets have been neceffitated to have recurrence, to an inverted collocation of words, a retrogradation of accents, an abfçifion of vowels, a detruncation of fyllables, and a diametrical aberration from all the legitimate modes of

speech,

fpeech, without the fmalleft relaxation of metrical rigour, repugnant and difcordant to the genius of our language, and of which there are multifarious exemplifications in the productions of the immortal Milton himfelf *.

### SECOND PHYSICIAN.

Good heavens ! what language is this? Why 'tis worfe than I could have imagined.

### CRITICK.

I told you fo, but you made light of all I faid.    Can any thing be done in this melancholy cafe ?  Had I not met you by accident,

---

* 'Tis worth taking notice of, that moft of the hard words in this fpeech are to be found in No. 86 and 88 of the Rambler, where Lexiphanes treats of Milton's Verfification, and profeffing his defire to be generally underftood, ftudioufly declines the dialect of grammarians, and if any where obfcure, begs it may be imputed to that *voluntary interdiction*.  I fhould be glad to know what dialect he writes in, or of what art thefe hard words are the proper terms !

The above fpeech, however, is faid to contain his real fentiments with refpect to rhyme and black verfe.

dent, I intended calling at your lodgings, to confult you on this bufinefs. And indeed had done it before now, but the adventure of the rehearfing poet drove it out of my head. I believe you like hard words as little as I do, nay, am told you have written againft them *. But you muft be fenfible, this inveterate difeafe, or rather epidemical madnefs, will not yield to that alone. More powerful remedies muft be applied, and I fhould be glad to know whether Apothecary's Hall furnifhes any antidote againft it. The ancients purged the brain of madnefs and choler, by means of white Hellebore: then why fhould not our modern Efculapiufes poffefs fome fpecifick to clear the ftomach and inteftines of the filth and trafh of hard words? for out of the abundance of the heart the mouth fpeaketh.

### Second Physician.

I know not; but I have a draught in my pocket here, I was going to carry to one of my mad patients. 'Tis a member of parliament,

* I remember to have feen a fmall treatife of that nature afcribed to Dr. Armftrong, how truely I cannot fay.

ment, who loſt his wits together with his place, at the laſt change of miniſtry. He has been very furious indeed, and we have had much ado to prevent his dying the death of an old Roman or modern Engliſh- man ; befides, he uſed to be continually raving about *Dubeity* and *Totality*, which he would have it, occaſioned him the loſs of his office. This makes me think, there's ſomething not unlike between his caſe and Mr. J-----n's, and that this potion may do our friend ſome ſervice, for I obſerve, ſince the mad member has taken it, he has been altogether ſilent as to thoſe hard words I ſpoke of. It works upwards, and with great violence. What do ye ſay ? Shall we try it upon Lexiphanes ?

CRITICK.

By all means. 'Twere to be wiſhed we could only recover him ſo far, as to enable him to tranſlate his own Ramblers into tole- rable good Engliſh ; ſuch Engliſh, I mean, as a common reader might underſtand, with- out the help of his dictionary. For, after all, this may be a bookſeller's project at bottom ; he might write his Ramblers to make a dictionary neceſſary, and afterwards

compile

compile his dictionary to explain his Ramblers. Such devices are not unusual in the
trade, and ought to be discouraged. Come,
Mr. J-----n, take this draught; drink it up.
'Twill be of mighty service to you, if you
knew all.

J ------ N.

Do not, Doctor, exhibit your medica-
ted mixture to me, but to that hypocrite of
learning to bibulate, who has manifestly no
skill in the politicks of literature, and who
thinks those who are endued with the out-
most rectitude of intellectual regimen, in
his predicated tortuosity, and inanity of
imagination. Like the Samian Sage, he
would obtrude upon me a quinquennial si-
lence *; and unless he be checked by a proper counteraction, would congeal me with
the frigid and narcotick infection of habi-
tual drowsiness, voluntary visions, invisible
rot of the mind, and secret prodigality of
being, into torpor of tongue, suppression of
sentiment, and inactivity of pen†. He sur-
veys

---

\* Almost literally from Lucian.

† Here is a *Quaternion* followed by a *Triad*. Consult the Rambler, No. 89, throughout, a most *delicious morsel* of Lexiphanick eloquence.

veys me with the microfcope of criticifm,
but my own laurels obumbrate me from its
fulminations‡. His cowardice is lured to
the attack, and he miftakes foftnefs, diffi-
dence, and moderation, for imbecility, de-
fection, and decrepitude of intellect. But
my firmnefs and fpirit fhall overpower his
arrogance, and repell his brutality. I fhall
convince him I have more fkill in the politicks of literature, than ever Vida had. And
fince my long and fatiguing fervice of celebrity, dazzles not the impertinence of his
intimacy to a fitter diftance, I muft confute
him with baculinary ratiocination. My cudgel, with reiterated repercuffions of communicated affaults, fhall foon diffeminate, by a
rapid eventilation, the brains in his pericranium, blood in his pericardium, marrow in
periofteum, and inteftines in his peritoneum.

## CRITICK.

So, he threatens with his cudgel. I thought
what 'twould come to. Doctor, fhall I venture on him? Will you ftand by me? You
fee what a fwinging fellow 'tis!

SECOND

‡ Rambler, No. 156.

#### Second Physician.

Stand by you! ay, that I will; and, in such a caufe, to the very laft drop of my blood. Courage, and to him again.

#### Critick.

What, Mr. J-----n, you thought to bully us, as you did Mr. Foote. In your cudgel, it feems, confifts all your boafted fkill in the politicks of literature. But you fhall not knock me down, as if I were your bookfeller *. Confider, my friend, we are two to one; fo not a word more of your cudgel Sir, as you tender your ears, or value going to fleep in a found fkin. You may chance to come off with a fevere drubbing elfe.

J - - - - - N.

* The ingenious Mr. Foote, it is faid, once intended to exhibit Lexiphanes on the ftage, in all the pomp and folemnity of his pedantry. An exhibition, which, in his hands, muft have been highly entertaining, and might have been ufeful. But he was deterred from it, on being told, that Lexiphanes threatened to appear in perfon, and perform the principal part himfelf with his Cudgel. The ftory of his knocking down the Bookfeller, who is crowned with the Jordan, in Pope's Dunciad, is well known. No doubt that gentleman regretted his *Pericranium* was not defended by that ufeful implement, when attacked by this Lexiphanick maner of reafoning.

### J - - - - - N.

Seeing I muſt ſuccumb under the violence of prejudice, the fury of force, and the ſuperiority of numbers, I ſhall protect myſelf with the maſk of deceit, the grin of irony, and the ſneer of diſſimulation *.

My very benevolent convivial aſſociates, I ſhall not henceforth attempt to darken gaiety, or perplex ratiocination by baculinary argumentation. Practiſe not therefore the inſtare of ſtrangeneſs, pronounce not the monoſyllables of coldneſs, but with the ſmile of condeſcenſion, the ſolemnity of promiſe, and the gracioufneſs of encouragement, attend to the ſonorous periods of my reſpectful profeſſion †, and concede me a more extended, a more deliberate, and a more favourable audience.

### Second Physician.

By all means. Speak, and ſpare not, my friend J-----n; words are fair, and therefore ought to go free. But fiſty-cuffs and cudgel-work is foul play, eſpecially among criticks

---

* A brace of *Triads*, which Lexiphanes is ſuppoſed to ſpeak aſide.

† Rambler, No. 194.

ticks and gentlemen.---'Tis heavenly fport, i'faith.    [*afide to Critic.*

### CRITICK.

I'm glad you like it.  But you'd foon change your note, were you to hear as much of it as I have done.

### J ----- N.

I will not indeed infift on the affirmation, that my Ramblers are devoid of defects; for having condemned myfelf to compofe on a ftated day, I might often bring to my tafk, an attention diffipated with the fhrieks and ejaculations of children; a memory embarraffed with heterogeneous purfuits, and inceffant interruptions from the importunity of duns, and fedulity of catchpoles; an imagination overwhelmed with the fumes of hefternal compotations of convivial Burton ale; a mind diftracted with a in agglomerating expedients to obviate the hebdomadal recurrence of the radical poftulates of my landlady's pecuniary impudence, and a body languifhing with diftemperature, confequential on the reiterated repercuffions of communicated pleafures.  But whatever fhall be the final fentence of mankind, I have
labouured

laboured to refine our language to grammatical purity, and to clear it from colloquial barbarifms, licentious idioms, and irregular combinations. Something I have added to the elegance of its conftruction, and fomething to the harmony of its cadence. And as it has been my principal defign to inculcate wifdom or piety, I have allotted few papers to the idle fports of imagination. Though fome, perhaps, may be found, of which the higheft excellence is to raife an undiftinguifhed blaze of merriment, eafy facetioufnefs, and flowing hilarity, for fcarcely any man is fo fteadily ferious as not to require a relaxation from the fternnefs of my philofophy, and the difciplinarian morofenefs of dictatorial inftruction *.

Therefore, Mr. Critick, I value not the infiduous faftiduofity of your reproof, an abdominal vociferation. And I obfecrate you, Mr. Doctor, to concede me leave of abfence, for I am, at prefent, inftigated by the ramifications of private friendfhip, to pay a biennial matutinal vifitation to my convivial affociate, the foul-harrowing Richardfon, the moft emphatical author of Pamela,

I                                    Cla-

* Ramb. No. 208.

Clariffa, and Sir Charles Grandifon, whofe
confort has for feveral periodical lunary cir-
cumrotations ceafed to be fluxionary, by
which means fhe has loft all her powers of
fecundity, and to the great infelicity of the
defiderating fair one, has become totally
unarable and unafcenfible *.

SECOND PHYSICIAN.

Worfe and worfe. I find I muft give
him a larger dofe than I thought on ; and it
may kill him, for I told you it works with
great violence.

CRITICK.

Faith give it him all. Though it fhould
kill him, there's no harm done. This fellow, if let alone, will poifon the fpeech of
the whole nation.

J - - - - - N.

I befeech you, gentlemen, to relax the
mufcles of your difciplinarian morofenefs. I
perceive that you are invidious of the high
feat, which my gigantick and ftupenduous
intelligence that grafps a fyftem by intuition,
has obtained in the pinnacles of art and lofty

* Literally from Lucian.

ty towers of ferene learning; that you are betrayed by paffion into a thoufand ridiculous and mifchievous acts of fupplantation and detraction; that you would gladly lure me into drowfy equilibrations of undetermined councils; and congealing my intellectual powers in perpetual inactivity, by the fatal influence of frigorifick wifdom, would deprive me of the ftamp of literary fanction, which my works have received from the diffemination of a rapid fale, and above all, from the annual emanation of royal munificence, the very mention of which muft drive competition into the caverns of envy, and make difcontent tremble at her own murmurs *.

### CRITICK.

What can the folemn fop mean by the annual emanation of royal munificence?

### SECOND PHYSICIAN.

What! don't you know he has a penfion † of three hundred a year from the privy purfe?

* Ramb. No. 190.
† Befides, being Lexicographer, Grammarian, Poet, Critick, Play-wright, Effayift and Novellift, all which Lexiphanes is to a very eminent degree, it

feems

CRITICK.

Where is the merit that entitles him to that rare favour and diſtinction* ? when you

ſeems he is alſo a ſort of prophet. At leaſt, I cannot help thinking, when he wrote his definitions of the word penſion, that he muſt have been under the influence of a prophetical ſpirit, if not the ſecond-ſight, for which, a witty but unfortunate man has ridiculed the Scotch nation, as being a ſuperſtition peculiar to them, though 'tis, in truth, a very ancient and univerſal ſuperſtition, many traces of it, being found in Homer, and ſome even in Shakeſpear. In the firſt place, Lexiphanes defines a penſion to be *an allowance given without any equivalent*, and ſecondly, *the pay of a ſtate-hireling for treaſon againſt his country.* Now I can hardly think that either of theſe definitions ever became entirely juſt, till Lexiphanes himſelf became a penſioner. For if his merit in authorſhip is the equivalent for his allowance, I make bold to ſay, that merit, if not negative, is at leaſt, to uſe a word of his own, entirely *evaneſcent*, and of courſe, no equivalent at all. In the next place, though it cannot be alledged he was ever guilty of treaſon againſt the conſtitution of his country, yet there are, in his writings, numberleſs treaſonable practices againſt its language, the purity of which, next to the preſervation of our conſtitution, our glory abroad and happineſs at home, is, methinks, the moſt important, and ought to be the moſt univerſal concern.

* I have heard it whiſpered, that the real cauſe which procured Lexiphanes his penſion, was the

con-

ſay he is not altogether void of ſenſe and
meaning, though frequently an odd ſort of
one, and always more oddly expreſſed, you
have

I 3

contempt and averſion he is well-known to entertain for the Scotch nation and their innocent country. It ſeems, the great man at that time was a-
fraid he might *conjoin* his *powers* of *altercation* and
*detraction*, to two very witty and ingenious men,
who, through caprice or faction, were then abuſing
a people very groſsly, whom, 'tis ſaid, they were
far from diſliking in their hearts. But this anecdote
is, methinks, extremely improbable ; for I can never imagine that a miniſter, who relying, it may be
preſumed, on the rectitude of his meaſures, and con-
ſcious uprightneſs of his heart, ſo nobly, I will not
ſay politically, neglected ſuch men as Wilkes and
Churchill, would ever ſtoop to purchaſe the ſilence
*only* of a Lexiphanes at ſo high a price : for I have
not heard he hath ever *employed his powers of celebration in the cauſe of his patron*, at leaſt I do not remember to have ſeen his very remarkable cloven foot in
the party wranglings of that period. Be this, however, as it will, it implies, at any rate, a very ſevere ſatyr againſt the taſte of the publick, which,
'twas ſuppoſed, could be influenced by any thing
ſaid on either ſide the queſtion, by that heavy affected pedant, who has not the leaſt notion of eloquence, poſſeſſes not the ſmalleſt talents for wit,
humour, or ridicule, but when he makes an attempt
that way, as do him juſtice, is but ſeldom, appears
as clumſy and awkward as a dancing bear.

have faid all you can with juftice fay in his behalf.

### SECOND PHYSICIAN.

Why, he tells you himfelf, his works have been *difſeminated by a rapid ſale*, and *his gigantick and ſtupenduous intelligence has obtained a feat on the pinnacle of arts and lofty towers of ſerene learning.*

### CRITICK.

Three hundred a year. Sdeath, 'tis impoſſible. It muſt be a lie, by all that's good, and I won't believe it.

### SECOND PHYSICIAN.

So! not fatisfied with giving me the lie downright, you fwear to it. Look ye, friend, 'tis nothing to me whether you believe it or no. But I tell you once more, he has a penſion of three hundred a year fettled on him for life, and I am not a perfon that like to have my word called in queſtion, when I affirm any thing in fo ſerious a manner.

### CRITICK.

Dear, Sir, I aſk you ten thouſand pardons. But let us have no quarrel about that.

No,

No, let us rather join in lamenting the melancholy condition taſte and writing are reduced to in our native country.

Fall'n to the ground, they can no lower fall.

'Tis really amazing our great men ‑‑‑‑‑‑‑‑ Yet, perhaps, I wrong them, they might give him this by way of huſh-money, to hinder his writing any more. ‑‑‑‑ That can't be true neither; he writes on, and what is worſe, they imitate him. ‑‑‑‑ Taſtc, genius, eloquence, even language are now loſt among us without recovery; we ſhall ſoon relapſe into that ignorance and barbarity into which the whole world was ſunk during the dark ages.

### Second Physician.

Do not deſpair; in a virtuous attempt, every means ought to be tried. Could we only cleanſe this Augean ſtable, whence all that filth and traſh has been ſpread abroad; could we drain this muddy ditch whence all thoſe torrents of hard words and terms of art have been poured out among the people, it might do ſome good. Were the

foun‑

fountain-head once dry, the ſtream would
fail of courſe.

### CRITICK.

Ay, as you ſay, every thing ought to be
tried, and no time is to be loſt. ---- Look ye
here, Mr. J-----n, we are very ſerious, you
muſt take this draught, indeed you muſt.
It will do you good ſervice, more than
you're aware of. Drink, Sir, and quickly
too, if you do not, we will gagg you, and
pour it down your throat by force.

### J - - - - - N.

You perſiſt with a moſt pertinacious ob-
ſtinacy, and the fury of your menaces debi-
litates my force, relaxes me with numbneſs,
and congeals my reſolution with the frigorifick powers of villatick baſhfulneſs, ſo that
I begin to queſtion the veracity of fame,
and almoſt ſlumber in the ſhades of neutrality *. But I am afraid the bibulation of
this antidotal mixture will ruinate me, and
that if I eject all my replendency of diction,
dazzling ſcintillations of conceit, regular
and unbroken concatenations of allegory,

per-

* Ramb. No. 159.

perturbations of images, figurative diftor-
tions of phrafe, foft lapfes of calm melliflu-
ence *, accumulations of preparatory knowledge, fudden irradiations of intelligence,
and powers of celebration in the caufe of
my patron; I am afraid I fay, that the annual emanation of royal munificence would
become torpid, frozen and congealed, and
no longer continue to flow with its accuftom-
ed accelerated velocity in its prefent eleemo-
finary channel.

SECOND PHYSICIAN.

He begins to comply; 'tis only the fear
of his penfion that makes him hefitate, and
faith, between you and I, there's fome reafon for it; had he written like a Swift or
Addifon, no-body would have minded him;
we have now got another tafte, we love thofe
who elevate and furprize like Bays. I think
we had better fpeak him fair, and flatter
him a little. --- Do; my dear J ----- n, take
our advice, drink this mixture, get rid of
that confounded abfurdity of hard words,
and learn to talk and write like other people.
All the world allows you a man of fenfe and

learn-

* Ramb. No. 152.

learning; and here's your friend, a mighty admirer of the sound philosophy and deep obfervation concealed in your Ramblers, would give almost any thing to see them tranflated into good old Englifh.

J - - - - - N.

Constrained by neceffity, inftigated by the ramifications of your private friendship, and overcome by the importunity of your folicitations, I declare myfelf obfequious to your councils, and behold I bibulate. ------ Good God, what's this? What a fortuitous collifion, what an inverted retrogradation, what an enormous combuftion, what an erratick grumbling pervades the total involuted feries of my inteftinal canal. I have affuredly fwallowed a fpeaking devil, or got a ventriloquift in my abdominal regions. Boax, Boax, Boax *.

* Vid. Lucian. The reader may reft affured, that after the fecond phyfician becomes concerned in the dialogue, moft, if not all, the hard words and Lexiphanicifms, put into Mr. J——n's mouth, are really to be found in the Rambler, though the references are neither fo numerous nor fo exact as they might have been, owing to a caufe already mentioned. Should any doubt my word, they may be convinced

with

## SECOND PHYSICIAN.

Well done my friend J-----N, ſtrain hard,
and you'll do the buſineſs.   Come throw up
*powers*, that villanous word *powers*, a word
never uſed by any good writer, but when he
ſpeaks of powers at war, or to that purpoſe,
but now applied by our modern fribbles
to every poſſible thing, to every thing re-
lating to man or beaſt, or to things in-
animate.   He hear of nothing but *powers*
of *ridicule\**, *mental powers*, *intellectual*

with ſome trouble, and add a thouſand more to the
ſtock if they pleaſe.

From this time forward, Lexiphanes is a mute
perſon in the dialogue; and I am perſuaded every
man of taſte, and well-wiſher to the language of his
country, joins me in the hope that he may ever continue ſo.

\* This expreſſion as well as *mental powers*, is to
be found in the *Dialogues of the Dead*; though not
in thoſe written by the noble author.   But then they
are in a manner ſanctioned by his great authority,
as well as by that of the honourable perſon (Mr.
Y—k) who uſes them; nor are the three dialogues
referred to at all unworthy of the place they have
obtained.   Notwithſtanding which, I make no ſcru-
ple to condemn theſe two phraſes as quaint and Lexiphanick.   Beſides, the word *powers*, in the ſenſe in
which I diſapprove it, is uſed even by my Lord Lyttleton.

*powers, patron powers of literature, pow-*
*ers of dolorous declamation.* Inſtead of ſay-
ton himſelf. Certain I am, if uſed at all, it has
been uſed very ſparingly in that ſenſe, by any of our
old writers. Yet I muſt own, the greatneſs of thoſe
modern authorities a little ſtaggers me, and makes
me ſuſpeſt I may have contraſted an unreaſonable
diſguſt at it, from its having been *hackt* about in the
manner it has, by our moſt affeſted authors, ſuch as
J——n and A——de. No man of faſhion is now to
be ſeen with a ſilver watch or buckles ; for this reaſon
only, the meaneſt of the vulgar, who can afford the
price, have got them, and they are univerſally deemed a piece of low finery. For the ſame reaſon, methinks, every polite writer ought to be cautious how
he uſes a word or phraſe, equivocal or doubtful at
leſt, and which has already been ſo much debaſed
by the common herd of ſcribblers.

I muſt likewiſe take notice in this place, that I
do not pretend to rejeſt or *expunge*, out of the Engliſh language, any, far leſs all thoſe words, which,
to preſerve the humour of the Dialogue, I have cau-
ſed Lexiphanes to throw up. Such a thought would
be highly ridiculous ; for experience and the practice of the beſt writers have ſhewn us that there is
no word, not even the hardeſt in all his Diſtionary
or Ramblers, but what may be proper, nay the pro-
pereſt at certain times, and in ſome circumſtances.
*Proper words in their proper places,* is the definition
of a good ſtyle given by Swift. Therefore it is not
the words themſelves, but their affeſted uſe, and
the affeſted phraſes that I find fault with. But how

to

ing, as people did formerly, fuch a one
is a perfon of talents, parts, or abilities,
the word now is, he has great *powers*, and
thofe *powers* are, according to the wares
he deals in, either *theatrical, comical, tragical, poetical*, or *paradoxical.* The modern
Rofcius cannot ftep upon the ftage, but in
the next news-paper, our ears are ftunned
with the *amazing theatrical powers* of our inimitable Garrick; nor M——y *exhibit* a new
piece, (another of their cant words, feldom proper, but in the mouth of a pup-
pet-man, which, however, they are fure to
*exhibit* on every ordinary occafion) whether
it be a *Defart Ifland* or the *Way to win him,*
but we have a difcuffion in the next review
on his *comick* or *tragick powers*, juft as it
happens to be written in blank verfe or
blanker profe.   In the next place, get up,
*gaze* I befeech you, *imp, prime, forms, honours*, great words with the mad poet; then
*take the lead* a vile phrafe, taken from the
Card or Billiard table. *Lore, Lore*, muft come
away

to attain the one, and to avoid the other, is not to
be learned from a grammar or dictionary; but by
keeping good company and ftudying good authors.

away next, a word of mighty requeſt in Pro-
logues and Epilogues to new plays ; if the
author has not been at ſchool, the audience
are deſired to excuſe his faults and pity his
ignorance of ancient *Lore* ; but if he has
dozed a few years at the univerſity, then
are they bullied with his tranſcendent ſkill
in Greek and Roman *Lore*. In the laſt place,
get up *gripe, growl, rouze, throbs, whine,*
words all of them Engliſh, but ſpoiled
Mr. J-----n, by your affected uſe of them.
So, ſo. Well done. *Heave* again, my friend,
put your fingers in your throat, I beſeech
you, my dear Sir, bring me up all your hard
cant words, of two and three, and if you can,
of four ſyllables.

J - - - - - n.

Boax, Boax, Boax.

SECOND PHYSICIAN.

Well done i'faith ; here comes *devoid,
delate, replete, ſuccumb, diſcuſs, torpor, fri-
gor, vernal, diurnal, paucity, inanity, vicinity, celebrity, hilarity*, and a thouſand others ;
ſo, ſo, his ſtomach at leaſt ſeems to be pretty clear now.

CRI-

### CRITICK.

I afk your pardon, Doctor, there are fome words yet, I infift on't, are not to be left behind.  He muft bring up *repugnant* and *abhorrent*.

### SECOND PHYSICIAN.

Good God, what do you mean? What are you doing? Why man, all thefe words are in the ·········· and ········

### CRITICK.

What's that to me? If they are there, I know no bufinefs they have to be there, at leaft on every occafion.  They fhall come up by Heavens, were they even in the thirty-nine articles.

### SECOND PHYSICIAN.

Nay, you'll do as you pleafe.  But take notice, I wafh my hands on't.

### CRITICK.

Here, get me a feather, that I may tickle his throat with it's *irritating powers*, and *refufcitate the convulfive motion of his epigaf-trial regions*.  So, here they come at laft, but one fhould think he wrote the ·········· himfelf, he had fuch an *abhorrency* at part-

ing

ing with *repugnant*, and so great a *repug-nancy* to part with *abhorrent*. ---- But as yet, I have seen none of his *verba sesquipedalia*, none of his words a foot and a half long, those I mean which end in *ation, ility, ality, utity, icitude, etitude*, and so forth. Besides, he has brought up none of his *Triads* nor *Quaternians*; none of his quaint affected phrases, such as the *silent celerity of time*, the *superficial glitter of vanity*, and a thousand more of the same sort. Should we leave these behind, he will be little the better for all the pains we have taken. Pray, Doctor, how do you account for that?

SECOND PHYSICIAN.

The most probable conjecture I can form, is what follows. These words and phrases, by their extreme *ponderosity*, must have sunk so far down into his *abdominal regions*, as to get below the *valve of the Colon*, and must now be entangled in the *involutions* and *rugæ* of his *intestinal canal*, in such a manner, that -------

CRITICK.

Ha! ha! ha! What are you turning a Lexiphanes too upon my hands? Come,
· Doctor,

Doctor, let us have no more of your medical terms and folemnity. They may do very well, and even be proper and neceffary in a treatife on anatomy, or at a confultation of grave phyficians: but here, between you and I, and on fuch an occafion as this, 'tis no better than downright *Lexiphanicifm*, what both of us fo heartily defpife.

## SECOND PHYSICIAN.

I afk pardon, I had forgot myfelf a little. Why, thefe words and phrafes by their great weight have funk fo low down, that they muft now lie beyond the reach of a vomit.

## CRITICK.

Then we muft give him a purge; or if you have ever a glyfter about you, I fhall ftand apothecary myfelf, though he fhould e'en ferve me as Gil Blas did his.

## SECOND PHYSICIAN.

No, no, we muft not dabble any more with him at prefent That would infallibly put an end to him. Do you not fee, to fpeak in his own way, that he labours under great *imbecillity*, that he is in a ftate of

K.                                    *debi-*

*debilitating exfudation,* that he is *relaxed with numbnefs,* and a *frigorifick torpor encroaches on his veins.* There is a *manifeft approximation towards the diffolution of his frame of mortality,* and whoever beholds him now, can entertain no *forgetfulnefs of the fragility of human life.* All thefe fymptoms

    With *mortal Crifis* do portend,
    His days to *appropinque* an end *.

To be ferious, we muft not let honeft Lexiphanes die of the Doctor, if we can help it.

### CRITICK.

Rot the fellow, were I fure this villanous infection he has brought in among us would expire with him, I would difpatch him out of hand. But you'll do as you pleafe.

### SECOND PHYSICIAN.

Well, I am told there is to be a fale of Authors and Criticks very foon; next week, I believe, at Langford's. I fhall be glad to fee both you and Lexiphanes there. Perhaps

* Two lines in Hudibras, who is painted by the inimitable Butler, as a great Lexiphanes.

haps you will be put up to fale yourfelves.
The time of auction will be advertifed in the
news-papers. If, however, you think our
friend's cafe fo defperate, that it will not be
fafe to wait fo long, you may bring him to
me to morrow morning, and I fhall then order what may be proper for him. In the
mean time, I leave you to inftruct him farther, in the beft manner you can. For I
am a little hurried at prefent, and am going, by appointment, to a confultation, with
fome other gentlemen of the faculty, on the
cafe of the Right Honourable --------- who
has got fuch an obftinate Paraphymofis,
that I fear we muft make a compleat Jew of
him at laft.

CRITICK.

Hark ye, Doctor, a word in your ear before you go. Could you not contrive to
mix fome of your potion flily in the great
man's diet-drink, for on my word, he ftands
as much in need of it, as Lexiphanes himfelf.
Would to God I had intereft to get you appointed Phyfician in ordinary to the -------,
and then, if you could prevail on them to
take your medicine, it would prove of migh-

ty

ty emolument to the whole nation; we should not surely have so many *tranquillitys* and *pacifications* and *unanimitys* in the next -------. But as for Lexiphanes, you may depend on my doing my best, seeing you have so well paved the way for me. Doctor, your servant.

And now, Mr. J-----n, the only and the best advice I can give you, however hard it may seem to a person of your years and conceited dignity, is wholly to forget, and even, if I may speak so, *unlearn* all you have hitherto been so fond of. Till this be done, you can never expect the sincere praises of men of sense, or the rational applause of the publick. The eyes of people, of youth especially, whose taste is not yet formed, and who have nothing to guide them in their judgment of books, may be dazzled for a while with the false glitter of your eloquence and the big tumour of your hard words. But how soon they come to be better informed, they will reject you with a loathing equal to that transport with which, it may be, they now admire and imitate you. Should the English be ever studied as a dead language,

guage, and your works reach to pofterity, if you are not reckonedthe firft corruptor of our tongue, they will affuredly look upon you in no other light than as an author who wrote in a barbarous age, when all true tafte in eloquence was utterly deftroyed. Thofe who make a foreign or a dead language their ftudy, are much better judges of its words and their arrangement, than of its grammatical niceties, or, if you will, purity. That Patavinity objected to Livy, by his cotemporaries, we can now difcover no traces of; but we hold him one of the chief clafficks on the fcore of his excellent words and compofition. Agreeable to this, and as I obferved before, the main excellence of a ftyle confifts in the choice of the words; the next in their order or arrangement; and what ought to be confidered in the laft place, is the grammatical conftruction, for none but a Pedant will be offended with a trivial flip of that fort, unlefs it be attended with obfcurity.

How it has happened I know not, but this order is now quite reverfed. You efpecially are faultlefs with refpect to grammar, even fo to a degree of pedantry; you have

K 3     not

not omitted a fingle *who, that, what,* or *which.* The placing of your words, may perhaps have fome merit; but then the words themfelves are execrable, and when they cannot be altogether condemned, your phra- fes are, if poffible, more abominable ftill. Nothing is fo familiar with you as the *eye of vanity,* the *hand of avarice,* with a thou- fand more of that fort. You have made a god, at leaft a perfon of every vice and vir- tue, of every paffion and affection: a figure of fpeech never, but fparingly and on very folemn occafions, ufed by good writers; whereas you bring it in, at every turn, a moft eminent proof of the utter corruption and barbarity of your tafte.

Would you chufe to forget all this fop- pery and abfurd ftuff? Would you wifh to acquire fome reputation as a fcholar and a writer among men of judgement? It is my advice to you, lay down an obftinate refolu- tion to read nothing modern, nothing that has been written fince the acceffion of the prefent family, unlefs by thofe authors who had formed their tafte in the forego- ing reign. Such were Pope, Swift, At- terbury, Bolingbroke, and a few more, to whom

whom I will venture to add, notwithftanding the high contempt you hold them in,
Buckingham and Landfdown. This contempt efpecially of Buckingham, which moft
of your brother Pedants * have joined in, I

* Mr. Warton, author of the Effay on the Genius and Writings of Pope, is the perfon alluded to
in this paffage. He feems, indeed, to have contracted a particular antipathy againft Sheffield, the
laft duke of Buckingham who had the misfortune
to be an author. He falls foul of him on every occafion, and tells us, *there is no ftamp of Genius on his
writings*, with other quaint ftuff of that fort. It is
He likewife, who adopts Mr. J-----n's opinion of
Walfh, and feems fo mightily pleafed with his calling that gentleman's writings *Pages of Inanity*, that
he puts I N A N I T Y in capitals. It muft be re-
membered, that Walfh was accounted by Dryden,
a good judge if ever there was one, the beft Critick
of his age; and it was He who in a great meafure
formed Pope, for which he celebrates him as the
Mufe's Judge and Friend, and for which his memory ought to be revered by every lover of Englifh
Poetry. Surely one fhould have thought that a
reputation, which Dryden and Pope, animated both
by friendfhip and gratitude, had exerted all the
charms of their poetry to raife, had been fixed on a
lafting foundation. But behold the inftability of human things! It is overthrown all at once, by the
great Lexiphanes, that invincible Drawcanfir; and
only by one of his hard words!

At

can account for no otherwise, than by the
ſtrong antipathy of bad to good, for none
have written purer Engliſh, and in a politer
ſtyle, whether verſe or proſe, than that il-
luſtrious nobleman. Not that I would ab-
ſolutely condemn all authors ſince that period ; ſome I know have undoubted merit,
and, had they not proſtituted their admirable talents to write for bookſellers, might
have been models of perfection *. But as

At the ſame time, and on the ſame occaſion too,
if I miſtake not, this Mr. Warton calls his friend
Lexiphanes the Excellent Rambler.

       Qui Bavium non odit, &c.'

  * I muſt own that the writer of a late hiſtory is
alluded to in this paſſage. And when we conſider
it, rather as the project of another, than the favourite
choice or theme of it's author, that he was writing
not for reputation only, but alſo from another mo-
tive, and moreover that he was limited in the time
of it's execution ; we cannot but ſtand amazed at
thoſe abilities which in ſo ſhort a time, eleven months
it is ſaid, and under ſo many diſadvantages, could
produce a work, of that weight and importance,
with ſo many beauties and ſo few imperfections, not
only an honour to it's author, but to the people
whoſe tranſactions it records. What a reproach is
it to the times it was writ in, that ſo noble a genius,
                      ſhould

none of them are, I'm afraid, altogether pure, it would be better for a perfon in your extreme ticklifh fituation of health wholly to abftain from them.

This being laid down as a preliminary, indeed, a neceffary ftep; you ought to betake yourfelf, without delay, to a careful and attentive perufal of the beft old writers. I would have you begin with the poets, taking care, however, to read them under the correction of a judicious mafter, otherwife you will be apt to make an odd inconfiftent jumble of poetick and profaick words, as I am fenfible you have already done. Were I to compare things fo wholly different, I fhould liken your Ramblers to nothing fo much as to the Pleafures of Imagination, and Young's Night Thoughts, both of them equally obfcure, affected, and full of hard words.

fhould either lie under the neceffity, or even find it convenient to write with any other view than reputation alone. It cannot, however, be denied, that there is fomething too fhining now and then, both in the words and diction; but with this effential difference; what is the fruit of art, labour and defign in the pedantick old fchool-boy, proceeds from inadvertence and want of leifure to correct in fo lively and fpirited a writer as Doctor Smollet.

words. However, when read with due pre-
caution, nothing can inftruct a man fo well
as good poetry, in the true fpirit of the Englifh tongue, and the force and energy of
it's particular words, of all which you have
hitherto been entirely ignorant.

After you have continued a proper time
in this courfe, I would advife you to betake
yourfelf, in the next place, to the ftudy of
our beft writers in profe, our divines, philofophers and hiftorians, fuch as Sprat, Til-
lotfon, Clarendon, Temple and Burnet of
the Charter-houfe. Obferve well their words
and phrafes, and all the different circumftances in which they ufe them. Take notice of
the peculiarities of their conftruction, and do
not reject them, though they fhould feem to
be not wholly within the rules of grammar.
Though I am fenfible that herein I differ
from fome writers, for whofe authority I have
the higheft veneration, yet I cannot help
thinking a living language ftands in fmall
need either of a grammar or dictionary.
The exiftence of either is plainly impoffible
before people have begun both to fpeak
well and write well. While they continue
to do fo, they are needlefs; and after a bad
taſte

tafte is once introduced, they will rather do hurt than fervice, at leaft, if we are to judge from your writings. The Syntax and choice of words are beft to be learned from good authors and polite company.

But. if you would fee the Englifh language in its full perfection, whether with refpect to purity, elegance, compofition, or choice of words ; would you fee a compleat variety of ftyle, whether on grave or ludicrous fubjects, read the works of Dr. Swift ; indeed, never lay them afide, let them never be out of your hand, but make them your conftant ftudy day and night.

And now being well purged, and in time, I hope, properly inftructed, to ufe the expreffion of an admirable author, whofe works, with equal pride and foppery, you have heretofore called *pages* of *inanity* ; if after fo much truely undeferved fuccefs you are difpofed

To launch forth agen,
Among th'adventrous rovers of the pen,

lay afide, I befeech you, that cavilling humour, that fupercilious vanity which leads you to pafs your affected cenfures on men of worth,

worth, infinitely fuperior to your own. Thinking, I fuppofe, that as much as you de-
tract from them, you add to yourfelf*. A-
bove all things, facrifice to the graces and

per-

* This difpofition is very natural to a Lexiphanes,
and almoft infeparable from his character. The
fame turn of mind which leads him to differ fo much
from the common and ordinary way of expreffion,
whether in fpeech or writing, leads him to look
down upon and defpife the reft of mankind from
that airy throne which he has reared for himfelf in
his own fantaftick imagination. There can fcarcely
be conceived a more felf-conceited fop than the author of the Pleafures: at leaft, as he hath drawn his
own picture in that rhapfody. The haughty over-
bearing temper of that perfon, who fo well deferves
the name I have given him, is univerfally known.
A moft eminent proof of it is his contemptuous
treatment of the late Mr. Churchill, a man with all
his faults of undoubted genius, and who, as a writer,
had much more merit, and hath fhewn an infinitely
better tafte than the pedant who fo arrogantly affected to defpife him. Had he not been fnatched away
by an untimely fate, and had he been more difficult
and correct, and learned to polifh and blot, methinks he was able to give perfections to rhyme it
has hitherto been thought unfufceptible of, and
which Dryden himfelf has not attained to; I mean
that of running the lines into one another with eafe
and gracefulnefs, and giving it all the variety and
fwelling periods of profe.

perfpicuity, both of which you have hitherto neglected, efpecially the former. When
you fit down to write any thing, digeft it
well in your mind, and lay down a regular
plan of it before you begin. Let your ftyle
be plain and fimple, fuited to your fubject,
and to the capacity of thofe for whofe perufal it is intended. But above all things, a-
void the rock you have formerly fplit on, I
mean, hard, long-tail'd words, and terms of
art. Give none of them admittance into
your future writings, unlefs only in fuch
cafes, for poffibly fuch may happen, where
the avoiding them would appear from the
natural poverty of our language, greater
affectation than the ufe of them.

I fhall conclude what I have to fay to you
on this head, by enforcing my own opinion
with

Perhaps Mr. Churchill was fufficiently avenged
of Mr. J-----n, for all the contempt He expreffed
for him, whether real of pretended, by the fingle
nickname of *Pompofo*; a nickname fitting him fo ex-
actly, that I had once thoughts of publifhing this
Dialogue under that title, as it would be more generally underftood, and is more familiar to our ears.
However, *Lexiphanes* is by far more pointed and direct, for it literally fignifies *Word-fhiner*, or one who
always ufes, and is mighty fond of, what my Lord
Lyttelton would call, a *fhining affected diction*.

with the authority of two of the greateſt wits
that ever were in the world, the one of modern, the other of ancient times ; I mean
Lucian and Swift. It gives me concern I
am obliged to mention to you Dr. Swifts
definition of ſtyle, which is, *proper words
in their proper places*, the conciſeſt, and, at
the ſame time, the fulleſt that ever was given of ſo complex a theme. I leave it to
your warmeſt admirers, and to yourſelf,
when ſober, to determine in what ſubject
you can find *proper places* for your hard
words, terms of art, and abſurd phraſes.
Surely no one will find them proper in weekly Eſſays, on popular ſubjects. I beg leave
to recommend to your moſt careful peruſal,
that great author's Letter to a young gentleman on his entering into Holy Orders,
which, if any thing can, will cure you and
thoſe numbers afflicted with the ſame diftemper of their preſent madneſs. The next
is the admirable Lucian, who gives an advice, which, though applied by him to hiftorians only, is equally applicable to all o-
ther ſubjects, and holds equally juſt in every language. 'Tis a general, an univerſal
rule, againſt which no exception can be imagined

gined, and, indeed, ought to be written in letters of gold on the moſt conſpicuous place, in every library and repoſitory of learning. It is this, *uſe ſuch words only as ſhall be well approved of by the learned, and eaſily underſtood by the vulgar.*

Should you again cheriſh an ambition to inſtruct and amuſe the publick with periodical Eſſays, or to tranſlate into good plain Engliſh, ſome of thoſe few Ramblers whoſe matter may render it worth the trouble; in the firſt place, make yourſelf maſter by repeated readings of the ſtyle and manner of the Tatlers, Spectators and Guardians, the only perfect models of ſuch way of writing, perhaps, in the world. But before you venture it to the preſs, read your Eſſay to ſome old woman, were it your landlady or bedmaker, and if ſhe does not underſtand every word of it, conclude there is certainly ſomething wrong, and never ceaſe altering it till ſhe does *.

---

* Doctor Swift ſtrongly recommends this method in the letter quoted above, and enforces it by the example of the famous and virtuous **Lord Falkland**, in the time of Charles the Firſt, whoſe conſtant practice, he tells us, it was, " when-
" ever he doubted whether a word were per-
fectly

Should you undertake a work of greater importance or of longer breath, after 'tis

perfectly intelligible or no, to confult one of his Lady's Chambermaids, (not the Wating-woman, becaufe it was poffible fhe might be converfant in romances,) and by her judgment was guided, whether to receive or to reject it. And if that great perfon," continues the Dean, " thought fuch a caution neceffary in Treatifes offered to the Learned World, it will be fure, as proper in fermons, where the meaneft hearer is fuppofed to be concerned, and where, very often, a Lady's Chambermaid may be allowed to equal half the congregation, both as to quality and underftanding." The opinion of this great mafter, with refpect to fermons, it is evident may be applied with equal force and juftice to weekly Effays, intended for the amufement of tea-tables, and inftruction of the youth of both fexes. It is with fincere pleafure I own that the *World* and *Connoiffeur* feem to be altogether faultlefs in this point. But Mr. Hawkefworth, a very ingenious man, appears to have fpoiled his *Adventurers* almoft intirely, by a fond and foolifh imitation of this Pedant, whom he equals in every thing where the other moft excels, and is far his fuperior in fancy and invention. His words indeed are not fo execrable, but his phrafeology is very little better, and he deals almoft as deep in *Triads* and *Quaternions*. I had not the *Adventurer* by me, when compofing the *Rhapfody*, neither did it occur to me, otherwife it muft have appeared at the bottom of the page, for I find it would have furnifhed me with many *delicious morfels of Lexiphanick eloquence.*

The

compleated, let it lie by you for some time, at leaft, till the felf-applaufe naturally at-

L tending

The inimitable Moliere too, an authority the greateft that can be alledged, conftantly followed the practice of Lord Falkland, recommended by Swift. It is a well known ftory of him, that he never ventured any of his pieces on the ftage, till he had firft confulted his old Houfe-keeper, to whom he ufed to read his comedy, as fhe was fitting at the fire-fide in the evening, at work, with her fpectacles on: and he always ufed to judge of the reception his play would meet with from the audience, by the impreffion it had made on the old woman, and he feldom, if ever, found himfelf miftaken. It would be well if our modern play-wrights, thofe belonging to the Inns of Court in particular, would take the opinion of their bed-makers and laundreffes, before they carried their pieces to the managers or actors, for of the two I take the former to be infinite-ly the better judges: and I fhould entertain much more fanguine hopes from a dramatick performance, at which a laundrefs, on hearing it read, had either laught or wept, provided however fhe had not laught at the fuftian of a tragedy, or cried at the dullnefs of a comedy, than from another over which fhe had fallen afleep; though the latter were to be fet off with all our *inimitable Garrick's managerial arts, theatrical powers,* and *judicious caft of parts,* cant phrafes in vogue at prefent; nay, even though it were to be ufhered in by a moft excellent prologue, and difmiffed with a ftill more excellent epilogue, both written by that gentleman.

tending the heat of compofition be wholly
abated. Then take it up, read it over in a
cool moment, refining, correcting, and po-
lifhing, to the utmoft of your power. But do
not truft to your own judgment alone. Confult fome friend, whofe candour and honefty
you can rely on. But let it be one who
laughs at your prefent manner of writing,
as heartily as I do. You cannot depend on
the opinion of your former admirers, or of
the great men who gave you the penfion.
Thofe who could praife or reward you for
what you have hitherto done, are, affure
yourfelf, very incapable judges.

And now when you have fet the laft hand
to your work, publifh it boldly. If you
fhould not chufe to run any rifque yourfelf,
or be at the trouble to follicit a fubfcription,
put it up to auction among thofe who deal
in buying and felling books, and difpofe of
it to the higheft bidder, not in the leaft re-
garding any character one of thofe tradefmen.
may have over another, for his own fuperior judgment, or the goodnefs of his wares.
A work of real and tranfcendent merit will
make its way into the world, though expofed to fale on the meaneft ftall in Moor-
fields.                                        But

But the laft, though not the leaft important advice I fhall give you, is this.   Have no manner of dealing or concern with bookfellers, except what I have juft now hinted at.   Never confult them, or take their directions about any fubject you are to write on ;  never contract or enter into any engagement with them about any work whatfoever; if you are unhappily under any fuch contract, at prefent, get rid of it as quick as you can ;  for it is impoffible that a man who writes for bookfellers, fhould write well. They do not expect, or even defire he fhould. They are like thofe builders who build on fhort leafes, and want their edifices to laft only for a certain term.   In my confcience, I believe they are the great patrons of long *vermicular* words ;  for this reafon only, that they blot more paper, and encreafe the price of their wares. In fhort, never fhew the bookfellers a manufcript, till you think it fit for the prefs, and then talk with them about nothing elfe, except the price they will give you for it.

Befides,  having now got a handfome penfion, you lie no longer under any need of writing for money.   But improbable as it may be, fhould you even be deprived of this provifion for life, do any thing; die, ftarve, perifh, fooner than proftitute your pen for hire, a dirty inftrument in ftill dirtier hands, to fpoil the language and corrupt the tafte of a people, fo rich and famous, fo renown'd and flourifhing, the mafters of the ocean and arbiters of the world.

Thus, Mr. J-----n, have I given you my beft advice. If you follow it, your Ramblers may poffibly be forgotten, at leaft, fo far as never to rife up in judgment againft you, and you may in time acquire a reputation which may chance to be lafting. If you do not, but return like the' dog to your vomit, and like the fwine, to wallow in the mire and filth of your hard words and abfurd phrafes, I can only fay, that I have acted the part of a friend towards you, and that you will have nobody to blame but yourfelf. But whatever courfe you follow, be affured that it is impoffible you fhould write worfe than you have hitherto done.

POST-

# POSTSCRIPT.

THE foregoing advice, tho' addreſſed to Lexiphanes only, and in a manner applied to one in his particular ſituation, is intended for all who may write for the future, and may, without any vanity I ſpeak it, if ſtrictly followed, be eminently uſeful to them all. It is, indeed, little more, the change of circumſtances allowed for, than a literal tranſcript from Lucian. And there is nothing in it, but what may be fairly deduced from him, unleſs it be thoſe paſſages concerning Bookſellers, who are certainly a very different ſort of gentry at preſent, from what they were in his time: owing to one of thoſe changes which the art of printing has introduced into the ſtate of Letters, and which, this in particular, is by no means advantageous to them. Lucian, were he now alive, would have been, I am convinced, of the ſame opinion, and would have concurred in the ſame advice.

L 3

In

In fhort, I have fcarce deviated in any one article from Lucian's plan, or made any additions to it, except in the Epifode of the *firft Phyfician*, or the *mad rehearfing Poet*, as I call him. I thought fomething of this fort abfolutely neceffary for compleating my defign, and I wanted to give my opinion, in the prefent difpute, about blank verfe and rhyme. A very great Philofopher and Hiftorian (Mr. Hume) exprefsly fays, that in all nations and languages, Poetry has attained to its perfection before Profe; and as far as I am able to judge, he is juftified in thefe fentiments by experience itfelf. For the fame reafon, whatever that may be, when we perceive the Poetry of a nation to decline, we may affuredly expect to fee, very foon, a like degeneracy in their Profe. Blank Verfe differing fo little by its meafure from Profe, naturally leads to a fwollen turgid expreffion, and a fet of Hypercriticks among us, ignorant of the general turn and bent of our language, and vainly fetting up Milton and Shakefpear, as models of imitation, who certainly fpoke a different dialect from what we do now a-days, and in all their truely valuable paffages, are entirely *unique*

and

and inimitable, have recommended this
Blank Verse, not only as the best measure for
Tragedy, where the example and success of
our most approved Dramatick writers, tho'
I cannot altogether condemn the rhyming
plays of Dryden and Lee, have rendered it
preferable, but also for the sublimest and
most ornamented epick, didactick and descriptive Poetry, for which it is altogether
unfit, unless when under the management
of a Milton or Spakespear. Thus has it
become fashionable, and hence the swollen,
turgid expression already mentioned, and so
natural and peculiar to it, and of conse-
quence, the vile affected Lexiphanick style
in Prose of Mr. J-----n, and his followers
and imitators. The conduct of the Dialogue shews, that the circumstance of the
*Pleasures of Imagination*, being the production of a Physician, is the reason why that is
pitched upon as the object of criticism in
particular, whilst other performances of the
same nature might have been met with e-
qually reprehensible. But though not one
tittle of the censure past upon it, ought
to be abated; yet, I think, a great
deal may be said in excuse of the author,

which

which at the time I did not attend to. 'Tis
certain, from the time of its firft appearance, it muft have been a juvenile performance, and the manner of it, as well as Philofophy inculcated in it, I believe were all
the vogue at the place where it was firft written, both of which are very dazzling in the
eyes of a young gentleman of a luxuriant
imagination, before he has corrected his
tafte from foberer and more approved models. Befides, from this *Rhapfody*, as far
as it is intelligible to me, he feems to be a
man of virtue and benevolence, a friend to
the natural rights and liberties of mankind,
and a perfon of an enlarged and liberal turn
of thought, qualities infinitely more eftima-
ble than the happieft poetical talents in the
world without them. Perhaps, the ftrange
and unaccountable fuccefs it has met with,
may be one reafon why his name ftill appears before it, though now of great eminence in a learned and ufeful profeffion.

' Having

Having here an opportunity, I fhall juft barely recapitulate what, after fo long an interval of time, I can recollect of the chief heads of my intended Preface, I mean the caufes of the prefent decline of tafte and good writing among us. The firft is that univerfal law of nature, to which all human things appear to be fubjected; namely, a flow rife and progreffion from a weak and infirm ftate, to that degree of maturity and perfection their nature is capable of, and thence a gradual decline, and total diffolution at laft. The illuftrious author, juft now quoted, has handled this curious fubject in his Effays, with all that accuracy and precifion peculiar to himfelf, and to him I refer the reader. My Lord Lyttleton has, I think, barely alluded to this caufe, but Doctor Swift has exprefsly taken it for granted. For he tells us, in his letter to the Lord Treafurer Oxford, that " the " *Englifh* tongue was not arrived to fuch " a degree of perfection as to make us ap- " prehend any thoughts of its decay." But I am afraid, that he was herein greatly miftaken. Setting afide Shakefpear and Milton, Poets *fui generis,* and of a ftrain pecu-

liar

liar to themfelves, it feemed, even then
paft a queftion, that the poetical ftyle had
been carried to its utmoft perfection by Butler, in the burlefque way, and by Dryden
and Pope in the grave and ferious, of all
whom we may truely fay, with Horace,

Nil oriturum alias, nil ortum tale fatentes.

And that Swift himfelf, and his cotemporaries,
had likewife brought our Profe to the higheft pitch of excellence it ever will attain to,
this is a manifeft proof; he lived to fee it's
decline, he lived to fee, not to mention
numberlefs other proofs, Gordon's ridiculous and affected tranflation of Tacitus, en-
couraged and fubfcribed to by all our prime
nobility and great men.

The next caufe which may not only have
haftened the decay, but alfo prevented the
due growth and full maturity of tafte and
Letters among us, has been the peculiar temper and fituation of our princes ; for nothing
is more true than this proverb :

Regis ad exemplum totus componitur orbis.

Of

Of all our monarchs that have reigned since
our tongue has become in any sort polished
and refined, none appear to have had the
smallest pretensions to taste, except the two
Charles's. The unhappy exit of the first,
and the violent troubles and convulsions in
which he was involved, during the greatest
part of his reign, account too sufficiently
why Letters did not flourish more under him,
and why he did not more encourage them.
The second was every way more fortunate.
bating his love of ribaldry and licentiousness,
then so prevalent in the nation, and attended
with such bad consequences, he undoubtedly possessed a sound judgment and discernment both in style and literary productions.
Even his short and *extempore* speeches to
his parliament, have a strength, and elegance, and dignity unknown to composi-
tions of that kind now a days. But then he
was entirely void of true generosity and liberality, and seems only to have had a silly
sort of good-nature which could not resist
the importunity of the many craving mis-
tresses and hungry courtiers about him.
Though no prince in his political capacity,
not even Augustus himself, was ever more
obliged

obliged to Virgil and Horace, than Charles was to Butler and Dryden, yet he had the bafe ingratitude to fuffer them, though both men of virtue and blamelefs characters in private life, the one to languifh in poverty and obfcurity, and the other to do what is as bad, to write for his bread.

I have fometimes amufed myfelf with imagining what a fortunate circumftance it would have proved for Letters, had our prefent fovereign appeared on the Britifh ftage, juft a century before he did. The declared liberality and protection of the monarch, would have infpired that manly wit and genius fo peculiar to thofe times, and made them foar to heights that now perhaps we have no conceptions of, whilft his virtuous example and avowed regard for modefty and decency, would have tempered their licentioufnefs, the only, at leaft, effential failing they had.

But, however, though Charles afforded no other encouragement to men of wit and genius, than his countenance, the notice he took of them, or the private approbation he beftowed on them, yet even that was attended with good effects, and produced very

happy

happy confequences. For if it did not create, at leaft, it encreafed an ambition in the nobles and great men, not only to patronize and encourage Letters more effectually than the fovereign did, but alfo to honour and adorn them by their practice and example. Nor did this *impulfe*, if I may fo call it, received from him, finally determine with him. It continued with the utmoft force and energy till the end of the queen's life. And, in fact, that whole conftellation of wits which fo nobly diftinguifhed and adorned the female reign, were all without exception, formed after the example, and even by the precepts of thofe that had figured in Charles's days. Such was Swift by Sir William Temple, Pope by Walfh and Wicherly, Bolingbroke, Atterbury, Steel, Addifon, Congreve, Prior, &c.

But now a race of foreign princes fucceeded to the throne, who having no models of polite literature in their own native tongue, could not be fuppofed to encourage what they had no conception of, in another which they did not underftand. But this was of little confequence in itfelf; for letters having never enjoyed more than the countenance

nance of the fovereign, had been long before deprived even of that; ever fince the
revolution; for William, though a great
man, and a friend to liberty, befides underftanding our language but imperfectly, was
as great a *Vandal* in tafte as the reft of his
countrymen.   But the fatal blow, was given
by the violence of the Whig faction, which
became then predominant; and forgetful of
the lenity wherewith themfelves had been
treated, and not contented with fhutting up
every avenue to preferment, whether in
church or ftate, againft their adverfaries,
attainted, profcribed, banifhed, and deftroyed them all as far as lay in their power; and
amongft them happened to be, not only
far the greateft fhare of the wit, genius,
and learning, then in the nation, but alfo
the moft munificent patrons, encouragers
and rewarders of them.   And this blow was
farther confirmed, and I may fay, altogether
rivetted by the long and abfolute government of a fole minifter, which foon after
fucceeded.   A minifter, who knew no method of government but corruption, no art
of perfuafion but proffering the dirty bribe,
and could lay hold on no one paffion or affection

fection of the human breaft, but avarice a-
lone, the moft fordid of them all. It was
no wonder that this man's adminiftration, e-
qually contemptible and inglorious, both at
home and abroad, fhould rouze up againft
him all the wit and genius, which he and
his faction had left in the nation. And it
was an unavoidable confequence, that He,
who had no tafte himfelf, as plainly appeared from the choice of his literary champions
and defenders, fo profufely paid out of the
publick Treafury, fhould be an irreconcile-
able enemy, and do all in his power to de-
ftroy That, which he knew was his mortal
foe, and which actually wrought his down-
fall as a minifter at laft.

Befides the long and inglorious continuance of this man in power, was attended by
another very pernicious effect. So violent
were the difputes and contentions raifed a-
bout him, and on his account, that the
whole attention of the publick was diverted
from every other object, and turned into
one channel, into that of politicks and party wrangling and altercation, producing only temporary pieces, which as foon as their
turn was ferved, were thrown afide like fo
many

many almanacks or new's-papers, and con-
taining only materials for inflaming the paf-
fions, without any of that rational amufement and inftruction which every man who
takes up a book, with an intention to perufe it, has a right to expect from it.

At laft, thofe party heats and animofi-
ties, having in a great meafure fubfided,
more from wearinefs and the want of proper
objects to wreak themfelves on, than from
fatiety or any other better caufe ; and all the
great men who had flourifhed in the queen's
reign, being either dead, attainted, retired,
or forgotten ; and during the ignominious
interval that followed, no capital work having been executed which might ferve as a
model of imitation, or great original and
natural genius arifen, whofe authority might
fix the attention and direct the judgment of
the publick ; it is not to be wondered at, if
in thefe circumftances fomething happened
to us, fimilar to that which befel the Romans when their licentious republick had
degenerated into a moft defpotick tyranny,
and all their party difputes and diftinctions
had been annihliated under the domination
of their emperors : I mean, that a parcel of
*Shiners,*

*Shiners*, and *Lexiphanefes*, and *Paradex-mon-gers*, fhould arife, and feizing an almoft empty ftage, by their vapouring and huf-fing, and that petulance and impudence, fo very natural to them, and by *exhibiting* fomething to the publick, that appeared *novel* and *brilliant*, in fhort, fomething that had not been feen before, fhould acquire a reputation, which, however, ill grounded at firft, may now be very difficult to de-ftroy. Hence the fame of an A-----de, of a J-----n, and many others, whom I fhall not, at prefent, mention. And hence the mo-dern reputation of a Young, who forgetting his better and chafter manner by which he had diftinguifhed himfelf, even when Steele and Addifon, Swift and Pope, were in the vigour of their faculties, became, in his do-tage, a perfect Lexiphanes, and fucceeded fo well in that way, that he is no longer known by his *Univerfal Paffion*, but by his *Night Thoughts*, at leaft his works are gene-rally advertifed under that title.

I have infifted the longer on this fecond caufe of the declenfion of letters among us, as it feems peculiar to ourfelves. I proceed now to the third and laft caufe, which is how-

M            ever

ever become univerfal. And that is the change
which the art of printing has introduced into
the ftate of letters, and which, as managed
at prefent, not only prevents their improve-
ment, but alfo their continuance in purity
and fimplicity, and even haftens and brings
on their degeneracy. It has, indeed, been
of the moft eminent ufefulnefs, by multiplying and difperfing all the ancients which
had efcaped the ravages of time and barbarous nations, as well as all thofe moderns who
truely deferve the name of Claſſicks in any
language, in fuch a manner, that their lofs
feems now to be impoffible, and that they
can only be deftroyed by the laft pangs and
dying convulfions of nature. But the change
which it has brought about in the trade of
Bookfelling, and alfo its having made Au-
thorfhip itfelf a fort of trade, have been attended, efpecially in this free and commer-
cial country with inconveniences, balanc-
ing, in a great meafure, thofe mighty advantages. Certainly, before the invention
of printing, Bookfelling was a very honourable and ufeful profeffion ; and at that time,
and long afterwards, it became ftill more fo.
Bookfellers and Printers, who feem then to
have

have been one and the fame perfons, were, in fact, the great reftorers of learning, and the moft learned men in the world them-felves, for the beft editions we have now of the Claffcks, and many other works, were publifhed, not only at their expence, but under their care and revifal. But tho' this profeffion may be fomewhat degenerated from what it originally was, and few who are now engaged in it may be fuch learned men and fuch capable judges of literary productions, as many were at the firft invention of printing; yet Bookfellers are ftill equally ufeful, indeed as honourable as any other merchants whatever, efpecially thofe who follow that occupation only, and remain contented within their former limits, or even when they proceed one ftep farther, and purchafe, at a price agreed on, the right of a copy from any gentleman who fhall offer it for fale to them. But when once they commence, not authors, but book-makers and manufacturers, literary projectors and undertakers, and for that purpofe hire labourers and journeymen to work under them, who are, indeed, very improper-

ly

ly ftiled authors, it is then that they become highly pernicious, and even entirely de- ftructive of all good tafte and learning.

In the firft place, the yearly, monthly, weekly, nay, daily lumber and trafh which they are continually difperfing; in immenfe loads among the people, under the titles of Journals, Magazines, Mufeums, Mifcella- nies, Records, &c. every one of which, ac- cording to them, contains more in quantity than another, and are all compofed by authors of the firft eminence; together with thofe innumerable hiftories and compilations of all forts, retailed every Saturday night in fixpenny portions, and that infinite variety of Dictionaries and Encyclopedias of Arts and Sciences, by which they fritter learning to tatters, and afford but an empty fuperfi- cial fmattering at beft; I fay, all thefe pro- ductions, which are projected and fupported, and even it may be faid, created by Book- fellers, are attended with this very bad con- fequence : That moft readers, feduced by curiofity, the perpetual puffing of News- papers, and a filly notion that the laft wri- ters on any fubject muft be the beft, their minds being clogged and vitiated with this garbage,

garbage, not only lofe all relifh of the old
approved writers, in which alone are to be
found the true and folid principles of learning and fcience, but alfo loath and reject them
juft as a green-ficknefs girl, when gorged
with chalk and trafh, naufeates the niceft
dainties fet before her at a regular meal.
And in the fame proportion, that the older
writers are neglected, modern original compofition is difcouraged.   For in the days of
our anceftors, every young writer who ventured a new performance abroad in the world,
which feemed to promife any thing, was always fure of, at leaft, one fair and impartial
hearing from the publick; and if he merited
the attention he claimed,  he met with his reward; if not, the worft punifhment he had
to dread, was being neglected and forgotten.   But We, their Sons, are grown much
wifer, as well as infinitely more cautious :
the greateft number now a-days, will not fo
much as caft their eyes on a new production,
unlefs, it may be, a Romance or a Novel
manufactured for a circulating library, till
they have confulted their monthly Oracles,
a Magazine, a Mufeum, or a Review, and
have feen what judgment is paft upon it by

M 3             • a Ma-

that Labourer whofe tafk it happens to be, or who has that particular branch of the manufactory, under which it falls, allotted to him by his mafter and employer, the Bookmaker. Further, from the characters of thofe who make up this periodical ftuff; for what man of any abilities, whether natural or acquired, will ever ftoop fo low, unlefs compelled by meer neceffity, when the concioufnefs of that, and of the unworthy manner wherein he proftitutes his talents, will probably render him a worfe performer than the heavieft drudge? and likewife, from the manner in which it is made up, always againft a ftated day which renders impoffible the obfervance of Horace's rule, not even *in nonam diem*, feldom *in nonam horam*, no alteration, no erazement, no rejecting, no waiting for the lucky moment, but away it muft come, generally as wet from the brain as from the prefs; from all which circumftances, I affirm, it is impoffible that thofe periodical publications can be other than crude infipid trafh, or elfe, what is worfe, vile affected Lexiphanick fuftian which diffufe and eftablifh a bad tafte wherever their circulation extends, and that may be called univerfal.                                    In

In the next place, by thofe arts and practices fo long continued and fo often repeated, the very name of *author* is become a term of ridicule and contempt. I doubt not but this very circumftance alone may have deterred many perfons of rank and fortune from appearing in that charaƈter ; together, perhaps, with their apprehenfions of the petulant ill-manner'd cenfures of our monthly Cricks. And here I cannot pafs by thefe gentlemen, without fpending a word or two on their praƈtices. They would fain pafs upon us as literary Doƈtors and Phyficians, as difcoverers of all defeƈts and imperfeƈtions in works of learning, genius and wit. I fhall neither difpute their pretenfions, nor queftion their fkill in their calling. But methinks it is fufficient mortification and even punifhment for a poor man, who fondly conceits the compofition he has juft put to the prefs will be univerfally read and admired, and excite the attention of all the wife and learned, to find it, when it comes abroad, lie uncalled for, and altogether negleƈted in his bookfeller's warehoufe. The natural death of all dull and unfuccefsful authors, is to doze away, infenfible, in a lethargy.

M 4 And

And this ufed to be their fate till that happy period, when bookfellers became book-makers, projectors, and manufacturers of lite-rary Journals and Reviews. But what fhould we fay of a Phyfician, who, after having paft fentence of death on a patient, and feeing him fall into a lethargy, a mortal fymptom, and the natural confequence of his malady, fhould be at great pains to awake him out of it, only to ftretch him on the rack, and make him expire in torture and agony; and then brag, as an inftance of his profound fkill in prognofticks, that no-body whom he had thus tortured ever furvived it? Poffibly we might not be able to controvert that fkill, but we fhould affuredly think him barbar-oufly and wantonly cruel.   Juft fo is the ge-neral practice of our modern Criticks.   But to return, that backwardnefs which men of independent circumftances difcover to ap-pear as writers, is of worfe confequence to Letters than may be imagined.   For whatever our Lexiphanefes and profeffed authors may fay to the contrary, I cannot help being of opinion, that the acknow-ledged fuperiority of the ancients over us moderns, is lefs owing to the fuperiority of

inde-

the languages they wrote in, than to that of their external circumftances; for they were almoft without exception, all of them men of diftinguifhed quality, fortune and confideration in the ftate, intimately converfant, and deeply engaged in the moft important publick concerns.

But I am infenfibly got into a fubject, and among a fet of company, Bookfellers, or rather Book-makers and their Labourers, very improper for the grave and ferious air which this differtation has hitherto affumed; therefore I fhall willingly take my leave of them at prefent, for befides purfuing the plan of this Dialogue fomewhat further, I have already handled them, in a fitter and perhaps a more agreeable manner, in another Dialogue, entituled, *The Sale of authors*, the hint of which, I need not inform the learned reader, is taken from Lucian's *Auction of the Lives of the Philofophers*, and which I may publifh alfo, fhould this attempt meet with a favourable reception from the publick.

And now having had occafion to mention the name of this illuftrious ancient once more, I cannot but obferve on the peculiar feli-

the

city that attended the Greek, the language he wrote in, which continued from his days upwards to thofe of Homer, and and we know not how long before, a period of at leaft a thoufand years, in a ftate of the utmoft purity. And I cannot, for my heart, conceive there is any extravagance in hoping that our own Tongue may be equally happy for as long a time, at leaft, as long as our ifland fhall remain, or our government fubfift in its prefent form. In fhort, none of thofe caufes which operated fo powerfully on the corruption of the Roman Tongue, and at laft wrought the deftruction both of that and the Greek, feem at all to threaten us. We have now a Prince on the throne, who is a Briton born, and who glories in the name, and we have the faireft profpect of an uninterrupted fucceffion of fuch Princes. Our government feems to be fixed on fo fecure a bafis, and fo equally balanced, that we have no reafon to fear its degenerating either into a Tyranny or Anarchy; and our fituation as an ifland, together with our almoft invincible power at fea, moft effectually fecures us from conquefts or invafions, or even hurtful intermixtures

mixtures with foreign and barbarous nations. So that it fhould feem we have nothing to apprehend for our language, but from our own levity and wantonnefs, our ridiculous fondnefs for vain and fantaftick ornaments, and a falfe brilliancy of ftyle. It was this which had crept into the Greek in Lucian's time, which begun the corruption of the Roman Tongue, and which now threatens to corrupt our own. But feeing that in glory and renown, and almoft in extent of dominion, we rival the Greeks and Romans, and excel them far in the wifdom of our laws, and in the conftitution of our government, methinks it fhould be the conftant ambition, and it would be a laudable one, of our princes and great men, and all thofe whofe fuperior talents and fituation in life enable them to guide and direct the tafte of the publick, to manage it fo that we might continue to rival them alfo in Letters and in Arts, which we can never expect to do, but by preferving our language pure and uncorrupted.

I fhould

I fhould now take my leave of Doctor J-----n, a title which it feems has been lately conferred upon him in the News-papers, and is, indeed, a very good name, either to travel with or advertife by. But fome of my friends have infifted upon it, in a very peremptory manner, that after fo much gravity and fo-lemnity as is difplayed in this Poftfcript, and in the Advice or rather Sermon addreffed to all authors in the perfon of Lexiphanes, I fhould adopt the practice of a certain judi-cious Critick and Manager, whofe invaria-ble rule it has been, after having exerted all his *tragical powers* in the *exhibition* of any of thofe *deep diftrefsful dramatic pieces* which he has fo charitably midwifed into the world, to difmifs his audience in good humour at laft, and to banifh all thoughts of hanging, drowning, or fhooting, which fo many in this country are apt to entertain without any provocation at all, by a moft witty and face-- tious Epilogue of his own compofing. They have likewife enforced this advice, by an authority, the greateft to me in the world, I mean by the example of my own hero, Doctor J-----n himfelf, who frequently qua-lifies the *fternnefs of his Philofophy*, and the

have

*difciplinarian morofenefs of his dictutorial in-
ftruction* with the *irrefiftable charm of eafy
faceticufnefs and flowing hilarity.*

In fhort, they have made it a point with
me, that after fo much formal gravity, I
fhould *exhibit all my powers to kindle up fuch
an undiftinguifhable blaze of merriment, and
raife fuch an unintermitted ftream of jocularity;
as to convulfe a large company of readers with
univerfal laughter, and make them difturb
whole neighbourhoods with the vociferations of
their applaufe.*

But alas! I poffefs no fuch *powers of
merriment* and *hilarity*; nay, I am really
afraid, that the following Letter, which fell
accidentally into my hands, and which I
have inferted at their requeft, tho' againft
my own judgment, will produce effects
quite contrary to what they are pleafed to
expect from it. At leaft I can fafely fay it
had fuch upon myfelf: for, as there is no
reafon to call in queftion the genuinenefs
and authenticity of it, nothing, I think,
can raife the indignation of any man who
has the leaft fpark of good-nature and humanity in his bofom, fo much, as to find
that a worthy and ingenious foreigner, who

and

has lately come to refide among us, and who has done us the honour to ftudy our language, in the fame manner as the moft learned men in all ages have ftudied the Greek and Latin, fhould have been fo barbaroufly and inhofpitably treated by us; and that for no other reafon, but becaufe he has unluckily miftaken Doctor J-----n's real aim and intention in compiling his Dictionary, and has thought he was learning from thence the real and fimple meaning of our moft common Words and Terms, whilft the Doctor was only difplaying his own great wit and ingenuity, his difinterefted patriotifm, and fincere love for his country.

I fhall make no farther remarks, though there is an ample field for them; but leave the unfortunate gentleman to ftate his own cafe, and to fpeak for himfelf.

The Letter above-mentioned was directed to a Gentleman of great eminence in the Law, whofe name I am not at liberty to reveal. It is as follows, *verbatim et literatim.*

MONSIEUR,

ME be one Franchéman dat repreſenté my grievance to you vor de adviſe. My occupation be to dreſſé and to frizé de Hairs of de Ladies and de Jentilmans; and out of de pure affection vor de bon peuple of Englandé, and vor deir grand improve-ment, and dat dey make de better appear ance, me leave my chere patrie, and come over heré. And me ave at de grand de-penſe made one purchaſe of de Dictionaire of de Docteur S----l J-----n, vor apprendre more facilement, and parlé more juſtement and proprement de Engliſh Tongué. But dat vilain Dictionaire ave ledé me into ver grand miſtaké, and ave goté me kické, cuffé, beaté, and my teet drivé down my troaté; and now me vant to know veder me can ave de action of de law vor my domage againſt dis Docteur J-----n.

Ave de patience, Monſieur, and me vill tellé you all my misfortune. Ven me arrivé a Dover, me ave dans ma poche one piece of de fine Bruſſel Lacé, as a preſant vor Ruffle, or oder tings, vor my ver good friend

friend Madame la Ducheſſe of -------. But no ſooner me ſet footé on ſhoré, but de grand vilain come, and he do ſearché me, and he take from me my Lacé. I aſké him, Foutre, vat Diable be you, and vor vat you robé me? He tellé me, he be one Officier of de Exciſe, and he do no more dan his duty. Den I ſay, Foutre, dis be de hateful Taxé levied upon de Commodité, and you be de Vretché hiré by doſe to vom Exciſe be payé. Den he enter in a grand colere, and he ſtriké me, and breaké my headé, Jarnie. I tella him, All dat be in the Dictionaire of de Docteur J-----n * ; but he damn Me, and de Docteur J-----n bot.

Ver vell, dus I loſé my Lacé, and ave my headé broké ; and now I go vor Londres in de Diligence, and de ver next day go to Monſieur S A Y, and deſiré Him to put in de Gazetteer, as one Article of Nouvelles ; Dat laſt nighté arrive from Parie, Monſieur Dugard de Belletête, to dreſſé and to frizé de Hairs of all his ver good friends

EXCISE, A hateful tax levied upon Commodities, and adjudged not by the common judges of property, but wretches hired by thoſe to whom exciſe is paid. JOHNSON's DICTIONARY.

friends de Nobleſſe of Englandé, dat he
ave his habitation at de Gridiron, in Broad
St. Giles's, and dat he vill vait on de Ladies
and Jentlemans at deir own houſé. But
Monſieur S A Y tella me, ver civillement
dat he muſt ave de Money from me, vor dat
de Gouvernment chargé to himé, and make
him payé. Den I tella him, I ſee it be ver
true vat Doéteur J-----n ſay of you*, Dat
you be one Bougre of de utmoſt Infamie,
and dat you be one Vretché hiré to juſtifie
de Cour. Monſieur SAY demandé of me,
for vat I affronté him in his own houſé. Den
I draw my fordé vor my propre defence, but
Monſieur S A Y také my fordé from me Begar, and break it over my headé, and den he
and his Diable kické me down ſtairé Jarnie.

After dis, to refreſhé and recruité my
ſpirit, I go to one Beer-houſe, and do callé
vor one coup of Liqueur, and do enter into
converſation vit one Jentleman dat vas fum-
ing his pipé at de fireſide, and dis Jentleman ave but one eye, one legé, and one armé.
And de grand conteſtation and de ver high
vordé ariſe about de gloire of de grand Mo-
N                narche,

* GAZETTEER. It was lately a term of the utmoſt infamy, being uſually applied to wretches that
were hired to vindicate the Court.            Ibid.

narche, and of de Franché nation, and de Jentleman demandé of me, Vat I be? I tella him, I be one Marquis of France, and one Chevalier of de order of St. Louis; and den demandé of himé, Vat be you? and he tella me, Dat he be one Lieutenant of one man of Var, dat he lofe one eye at Cape Breton, one armé in the combat vit *Monfieur Conflans*, and one legé at Martinique, and dat he live, at prefant on his half-pay, and dat he ave, befide one fmall penfion of Tirty Livre fterlin a year. Den I fay to him; Jan Foutre, I be my own Matré, but you be one flave, hiré to obey your Matré; Doctor J----n tella me fo *, and dat you be one Traitre to your country Begar. De Jentleman fay noting, but vit his ftumpé knocké me down, and drivé tree of my teet down my troaté.

Ver vell, all dis ver vell. I lie one mont in my bedé, and ven I be recoveré, I fee one morning one avertiffement vor de Conumers of Oats, to meet togeder at de Sun-Tavern, Cheapfide, to confulté on deir fpecial

---

* Pension. An allowance made to any one without an equivalent. In England it is generally underftood to mean pay given to a ftate-ftireling for treafon to his country.——Pensioner. A flave of ftate hired by a ftipend to obey his Mafter. Ibid.

cial affairé. I confult de grand Dictionaire of dis Docteur J-- --n, and I fee dat Oats be de food of de horfé, in Englandé, but of de peuple in Scotlandé *. Le Diable, fay 1 to myfelf, do de Englifh h r̈ und de Scottifhmans meet and drinké togeder in dis country! Begar I vill go fee dis Mervielle. Vell, I go to de Caberet at de hour, and fee ver few Scottifhmans, and ver many Englifhmans, but not one Horfé nor one Maré. I vait long time, and at laft I fay to fome, dat I tought vere Englifhmans, by deir broad facé and deir great belly : Vat Jentelmens be all your Horfé fické, or take phyfické, dat you come here in deir place, and be de reprefentative of de Horfé, But dey tinké I do affronté dem, and dey d---n my eyes, and kické me, and cuffé me, and bruifé me fo, dat I be took up for deadé, and do keep my bedé ever fincé.

But, Monfieur my Apoticaire tella me, dat dis Docteur J-----n, be himfelf, ten timé one greater flavé to his Matré, and ten timé one greater Traitré to his country dan de Lieutenant of de fhip of Var vit one eye, one

---

* OATS. A grain which, in England, is generally given to horfes, but in Scotland fupports the people.  Ibid.

one armé, and one legé; vor dat he ave got one penfion of Tree Hundred Livre fterlin a year, vor de vriting of de nonfenfe and de grand ftuffé; vereas de poor Lieutenant dat lofé one half of himfelfé, in de fervice of his country, ave got but Tirty. Derefore, Monfieur, mon Cher Ami, I befeecha you to filé one billé in Chancery againft dis faid Doûteur S----l J-----n, vor dat He, vit his vilain Diûtionaire, vilfully, and vit malice propenfe, ave cheaté, deceivé, and abufé me fo, dat I ave got my headé and fordé broké, my teet knocké down my troaté, and myfelf fo kické, cuffé, and bruifé, dat I keep my bedé, and ave lofé all my time and bus'neffé; and dat you vill obligé him, de faid Doûteur S----l J-----n, to make com- penfation fufficient to me, vor all my do- mage, out of de pay givé to himé, as hire- ling of de ftate vor treafon to his country, and to demandé my pardon in de publique papier, and likevife, to make de neceffaire changé in his Diûtionaire.

*I ave de Honeur to be,*
*Vit all Refpeût poffible,*
*Monfieur, Your ver humble Serviteur,*

Dugard de Belletête.